Bishops Navy

Bishops Navy

White Knees of Hanoi Series
Book IV

By

A.M. Hamilton

To order additional copies of this book, contact:
Xlibris Corporation
1-888-795-4274
www.Xlibris.com
Orders@Xlibris.com
120055

Other books in the series

BISHOPS PACKAGE

BISHOP'S RESOLUTION

BISHOPS EASTER

By

A.M. Hamilton

First Printing winter 2012

Special thanks to Robert Pike for his contribution in making this book a reality. He is solely responsible for its content.

CHAPTER I

The H.M.C.S. Vergil, because Vigil had already been taken, was the name of the Crist Craft boat that Group 5 used to ply the waterways on. For more than a week the small craft had been secured to the dock in front of the compound and to keep the engines in top condition the craft needed a run. Lieutenant Scott had ordered a break from construction for an afternoon of basically touring the harbor. But to make the trip official they had to search at least one san pan.

With a stiffening breeze coming off the Gulf of Tonkin, the waters were choppy out in the main channel, but up between the land masses it was reasonably calm. This made Bishop somewhat appreciative due to his proneness to sea sickness.

Sitting in a seat beside Kirk the helmsmen Bishop pictured in his mind where the others were. Greg was the ships mechanic, or engineer and he was in the engine room at the back and Mike was the radio man whose position was below in a small cabin surround by radar, sonar, and communications equipment. They even had a small satellite dish radio for contacting the embassy when they needed to. The only problem was the other equipment required so much electricity that in order to use the dish they had to shut down all the equipment. In most instances this would be a problem, but the only need to use the dish was after they were alongside another ship which meant the other equipment wasn't necessary anyway.

Lieutenant Scott was in command and he stood beside Kirk on the so called bridge with binoculars in hand. Scott basically pointed to an object and Kirk turned in that direction. Voice command was needless when they were so close to one another. In fact, Kirk got so used to Scott's tactics that he usually made the turn before it was ordered.

Bishop watched the landscape roll by on a series of wakes and cross wakes that jarred the boat one way then the other. He noticed that the seamen were all wearing their respective sea caps, while Scott had on his dark blue beret. Bishop was wearing his new NATO blue beret that was the same color as the small ensign of the NATO flag flown from the main mast.

The mission, as it was logged in the book, was euphemistically called a sea trial and quick peek. This was the nickname for a high speed patrol and to search various vessels for contraband. The contraband was usually drugs or weapons being brought in by independent contractors, using their motorized sampans as a ferry service from larger ships far out to sea that could be as much as a hundred miles in some cases. This meant the mother ship was outside the range of the Canadian radar.

"Hey sir!" Bishop called over the sound of surf and engine noise.

"Yes Corporal?"

Bishop had been eyeing the different ocean going ships moored at different spots about the harbor.

"How come these ships fly so many flags?"

"The flag in the stern is the country of origin and the flag on the mast is the country that is protecting it. Like that one over there," Scott said as he pointed to a Russian freighter. "The Soviet flag is on the stern and the North's flag is on the mast."

"I got ya."

Bishop then started to scan all the ships that were present and noticed Hungary, Romania, Czechoslovakia, Russian, China, and even a French ship had made port.

"What about those tied up to the dock?"

"They don't have to fly a stern flag when they make contact with the dock. But they still have to fly the North's flag from the mast."

"What's so special about them?"

Kirk turned and said, "They're trying to hide something."

"So we're going to check them out right?"

"Nope," Scott replied.

"How come sir?"

"Because their under customs control eh," Scott replied. "We only have jurisdiction up to the time they reach port."

"So let me get this straight okay. We can search those ships out there that are parked, but not those already tied up?"

"You got eh," Kirk said with a grin.

"So what about all these little ships. What happens when we case one of these little shits and then end up hitting the beach?"

"Then local police take over. Even if they hit a reef, we can't go any further."

"Because their grounded on the reef?"

"Right again Corporal. You pick this up fast."

"Pick what up, a bunch of shit regulations?"

"Them's the rules, Corporal," Scott said firmly.

"Man they got more loop holes than a box of Cheerios."

"No lone ranger stuff out here Corporal. Everything by the book eh?" Scott said.

Scott was making sure the Corporal didn't pull any questionable offenses, like the one with the Vietnamese guard at Group 6 the day he and Wilkins went after the POW's. Tennyson had filled in the Lieutenant before they left to come back to Hai Phong and it was this premises that got the Corporal temporarily attached to coastal watch. What Bishop didn't know was, his trial had been early that week.

"Sir!" Mike called up, his hand reaching through a small porthole type thing in the instrument panel. It was the most direct route for messages.

Scott took the note and read it, then called down the opening, "Any of the Coast Guard close by?"

"Not responding sir!" Mike called back up.

"Right," Scott replied and then told Kirk to change course and head farther out to sea.

"What's up sir?" Bishop asked casually when he saw the bow swing around hand head out towards the horizon.

"Sampan in trouble again. Probably full of refugees trying to make for China."

"You got to be shitten me Ralph, that's a thousand miles away."

"Not really Corp," Kirk said. "See that big island out there at your ten o clock?"

"Yea so?"

"That's China."

Bishop squinted through the shine of mist that hung over the sea like a belligerent fog, and even though judging distance over open water was difficult, it did seem like a thousand miles. In actuality it was less than two hundred.

"You said the Coast Guard?" Bishop asked.

"Right, they're the ones supposed to be rescuing stranded ships, not us." Kirk said disgustedly.

"So why the fuck ain't they coming out there?"

"The North feels that anyone trying to escape in a boat should be left to drown." Scott said.

"Their tough shit for leaving?"

"Right," Scott replied.

"Should we break out the weapons sir?" Kirk asked, this wasn't his first rescue and he always felt better when they saw a pistol on his belt.

"Let's see what we got first."

Kirk nodded and increased the speed. The craft seemed to rise out of the water and just touch the top of each wave. It felt very exhilarating and Bishop's sense of nausea dissipated with each bounce.

*   *   *

It wasn't that big a ship, something on the size of a Great Lakes fishing boat. It was of the open hull design and a small wooden cabin directly over the stern was used as the bridge and wheel house, and only had room for two. A large mast about twenty feet high had a small boom to it for pulling in fishing nets, but the age prevented anything like that from taking place. It was the human cargo that was of interest.

More than thirty people were jammed onto this floating wreck and had paid a great deal of money to get out of the clutches of the North. They had left before dawn from Cat Bo Island into gradually increasing surf. The ship normally would hold several tons of fish, so the number of men, women, and children wasn't the source of the low riding hull. It was all the leaks that made the boat look like it was sinking.

When the H.M.C.S. Vergil arrived the escape ships engine had stalled due to water getting into the gas tank. Huddled together like frozen fish, the people had expressions of dread as they contemplated being returned to the North. They knew they probably would be shot as dissidents. But the appearance of the Canadian's all had them staring at the four man crew.

Kirk brought the Vergil within 50 feet of the derelict, just close enough to talk but not touch the boat.

"Captain!" Scott called out in Vietnamese. He had learned enough of the language to get some idea of what was going on and because interpreters couldn't be trusted.

"You help!" came the reply from a short oily looking man by the wheel house.

"What wrong?"

"Gas no good, water inside."

"Engine good?"

"Yes!"

It was then Mike stuck his hand out the slot to had Bishop a note. The Corporal read it out loud to the officer who was standing by the railing.

"Contact at 128 degrees 40 miles sir!"

Scott came back to the bridge and stuck his head into the small radio room.

"Chinese?"

"Possibly sir, their speed is twenty two knots that's what their patrol boats do."

"How long?"

"About two hours in this surf sir."

"How far are we from the international line?"

"About a quarter mile as I make it."

Scott stood erect and grabbed his binoculars; he looked in the direction of the approaching vessel. It was still too far off to identify precisely and the waves splashing over the bow made it even harder to determine the exact distance. One thing was certain, it was in a hell of a hurry to get out to them.

"Another target sir!" Mike called out, this time he didn't need to write it out.

"Where!" Scott called.

"280 degrees speed 46 knots. I think it's the hydrofoil sir."

Scott wheeled around and looked toward Hai Phong eleven and three quarter's miles to the northwest.

"Black hats approaching everyone get a side arm!" Scott called out.

The black hats were the North's coastal patrol unit assigned to the small Navy. There were no large ships in the inventory, mostly high speed patrol boats that they got from the Russians. The boats themselves had been bought from an ocean racing company in California.

"They're about ten minutes away sir," Mike called out as he drew his pistol from a small cabinet and put the holster on over his chest. The pistol hung down under his arm pit like the type detectives wear. This was how all the pistols the crew wore were positioned.

In seconds Bishop and Kirk were armed and standing by the helm. Scott was handed his pistol and holster as Greg came up from below and the crew were now at combat stations. All the men stood ready and looked toward the harbor where they could see the foam flying out from under the approach craft as it skipped across the waves like a low flying airplane.

"Now what sir?" Bishop asked.

"Okay, everyone raise their right hand!" Scott called out.

"What the fuck for?"

"Just do it Corp," Greg said, and Bishop complied.

"Repeat after me, I swear I didn't see anything!" Scott ordered.

The men in unison swore the oath.

"Right, Greg bring up that can of gas, the one in army paint. Bishop go help him."

Kirk brought the boat closer to the vessel but kept about ten feet away.

"Don' touch the boat!"

"Yes sir I know."

It was a minor detail, but under regulations if a NATO ship comes into contact with a vessel it then has to defend the vessel from attack by anyone. Contact meant any form of touching if only briefly, like long enough to pass them a can of gas.

Bishop and Greg stood on the stern of their ship as Greg pulled up a grappling pole, the type with a hook on the end to drag things in the water closer.

"Ready sir!" Greg called.

"Pass it over!"

Greg then handed the end of the pole to the captain on the escape boat. Taking his end he slipped it under the handle of the five gallon can of gas and picked it up. The can slid down the pole to the opposite ship and one of the other crew members grabbed it, instantly taking it below to pour into the gas tank.

Kirk gave a quick goose to the throttle and the Captain let go of the pole as their ship bounced ahead. Kirk quickly stopped the boat about thirty feet away.

"I thank you good sailor!" the Captain called to Scott.

Scott gave a short wave and then looked in the direction of the North's boat which was now less than a mile away and closing fast.

"Better get those people covered up Captain or this is going to be a short trip for you.!"

The Captain waved and ordered the passengers to lie down on the wet deck. He and another crewman hauled what looked like a sail over the cringing souls an then a large net to cover a few that didn't completely disappear.

It was then that the hydrofoil arrived in a splash of glory. Once the ship settled back into the sea the wake dramatically increased so much so it created a small group of waves that washed water over the Canadians deck. Everyone's feet got wet and water swung down into the radio room. Fortunately Mike's body blocked the water from hitting the equipment, but a round of cursing came from the only man below.

When the North's boat pulled up parallel with the Canadians several sailors in black uniforms wearing black baseball hats came out on deck with automatic rifles in their hands. They lined up along the railing with one man standing alone on the stern. Then an officer appeared wearing a garrison cap similar to what the French Navy officers wore, only in black.

"Judas Priest, it's the snake," Scott mumbled just loud enough for Bishop to hear.

"Lieutenant Scott, you are a long way from your patrol area!" Captain Xiem called through a bull horn.

"Got a distress signal, thought I'd help out!" Scott called back.

Bishop was surprised by how well the captain spoke English. Probably another graduate from Edmonton, he said to himself.

It was then the motor on the escape boat sputtered to life as a cloud of smoke rolled over the small ship.

The Vergil was playing the role of the blocker craft. It was positioned between the North's ship and the escape boat. This meant that it was hard for the North to see what was going on with the smaller boat.

"Who are they?"

Scott looked at Bishop and said, "Remember your oath!"

Bishop nodded but said nothing.

"There fishermen from Hainan Island. Had some engine trouble but I think they got it working now!"

"Did you check their papers?"

"Yes sir, they are in order!" Scott called back.

Suddenly the escape boat roared into action and began heading for the open sea. The smaller ship bounced in the higher waves but managed to get a good rhythm up.

Kirk poured on the accelerator to keep them in the middle of the small fleet.

In Vietnamese the Xiem called for the escape ship to stop, but the trembling captain remained constant in his quest to get away. It was then the North's ship increased speed to pace the other two.

"Tell him to stop or we will fire!" Xiem called to Scott.

"I don't think he cares sir."

"They aren't fishermen they are smugglers of dissidents. Tell them to stop or we will shoot!"

A few seconds passed as the ships raced through roughening waters. They were only a few hundred feet from the international line and the escape boat was going to try and make it.

Xiem waved his hand and a short burst of automatic rifle fire including two green tracers whipped over the Vergil and impacted in the wooden mast.

The Canadian's instantly drew their weapons and Bishop dropped into the snipers squat with pistol aimed directly at Xiem.

"You put one more fucking round over this boat and I'm going to blow your mother fucking ass away, sir!" Bishop yelled.

Xiem yelled out something and the man who fired lowered his weapon.

"Control your men Lieutenant!"

"Not until you control yours Captain!

The ships ran on silently. Each officer was trying to stare down the other as they drew closer to the borderline. The intermingling wakes bashed the sides of the boats as if they were slapping each other into submission. On both ships the sailors watched for any sign of a fight, that wouldn't end easily.

"WE'RE OVER!" Mike called and at the same time Scott looked down at a small control panel as a red beacon light come on. In the North's ship they too received the international line indicator in the wheel house. It was a red light bulb hanging from the ceiling.

Xiem stubbornly turned and went inside his control room and ordered the boat to be put back to shore.

Bishop stood up and holstered his weapon and with a grin that spread like a rash across his face he said, "We fucking did it sir!"

The seamen gathered in the small bridge of the Vergil and watched as the North's hydrofoil went into a full speed retreat. Kirk slowed the boat and it came to a bobbing pause. They all witnessed the escape boat that was heading full speed in the direction of the approaching Chinese vessel.

Bishop could just make out a head coming up from under the sail and netting. Then another and another. Before it was too far to see, all the refugees were standing and waving back at him.

"What about them sir" Bishop asked. "Now they're a Chinese problem?"

"Not really Corporal. The Chinese like anyone who hates the North," Scott said as he slapped Kirk on the shoulder and the Vergil also retreat towards home.

CHAPTER 2

Horst was at his usual tea restaurant about two blocks from his apartment and had just missed a typical monsoon down pour. His cycle was at the curb with a spoke break attached to keep it from being stolen. With the increase in bombing a shortage of scooters was occurring to replace those destroyed. A black market price had tripled in only two weeks since Easter.

The view of the busy street filled with marketers left him feeling optimistic about the invasion down south. The news the war was going well made those at home seem more relaxed even with the increase of bombing raids by American Navy and Marines. The US Air Force had dropped back from their usual carpet bombing because large targets that required such effort had dried up. Most of the military bases looked deserted and it was construed by US defense sources that all of the military were down south and not in Hanoi any longer.

The Navy and Marines flew in two plane formations as hunters looking for what little meat was left on the bone. It had gotten to the point you could set your watch to the arrival of the twin plane attackers.

Horst was planning his day as he usually did at this time. He hadn't heard from Brown Shoes in a few days and his checking newspapers at the Polytechnic for any new information about missing persons provided no results.

On the other hand, he was getting attracted to a specific research student from Cao Bang Province who had an interest in photography. Secretly she told him she was interested in being a fashion model in Paris, but she felt she didn't have the right profile. Horst was trying to convince her that being a clicker was more profitable simply because a model may only have one session a month, where a clicker always had work.

It was then that Horst got the shock of his life. Rounding the open front corner of the store was Brown Shoes who had Werner in tow. As the two approached Horst leaned back in his chair like he had just been handed a death certificate.

"Good Got," Horst said as the two seated themselves. "Where the hell have you been?"

Brown Shoes held up his hand and ordered drinks from the waitress who noticed the inclusion of the guests to her usual lonely customer. She nodded and began to fill the request.

"It's none of your business." Werner replied.

"What the hell do you mean? Do you know how much trouble you've caused us?"

"He does have a point," Otto added in support.

"When generals confer with privates then I'll keep you in the loop."

Horst straightened himself in his chair. He knew his place now and didn't think it was a good idea to start a fight in the middle of a restaurant right in the enemy's living room as it were.

"So now what?" Horst queried.

It was then the drinks were delivered and the women left as fast as she arrived. Tipping wasn't expected by foreigners and that added credence to the phrase, 'cheap tourist.'

When the waitress was beyond ear shot Werner drew out two small note books, the size of small diaries. His jacket was damp and the impression of the books being inside still creased the fabric.

"These are copies of my field notes. One part of the book is half accurate the other part is wrong. You're to keep these for me until I ask you to send them on," Werner said as he handed a copy to each man.

"Where do we send them?"

Otto reached over and grabbed Horst by the arm. It was a gesture to keep quiet and let the man finish.

Werner took a drink from his glass of warm tea while the other two men starred at the small books. They didn't know what was inside or which part of the correct information they had. It was obvious someone back west would know how to put it all together, whatever it was.

Horst was overly curious and opened his book letting the white pages flutter together. There was no book mark so a specific page didn't present itself. One page did catch his eye and he held the book open. On that particular page was a chart of some kind. Several columns with amounts written in them.

Otto noticed it and reached over to close the book.

"No, you can read it," Werner said then added. "It's in code."

"What is this chart about?" Horst asked casually. "It looks like a bank statement."

"Very good, that is what it's supposed to be."

"I'm only guessing," Otto said. "But I think the numbers aren't supposed to tell a statement, but go with other information elsewhere in the book."

"Do you know how that would work?" Werner asked.

"I would say that the numbers in the chart correspond to blank spaces in your documentation."

"Very good, where did you learn this?"

"We, used to use something like it back in our days as dissidents," Otto said. "Remember Horst, when we gave coordinates or something?"

"Ja," Horst said, then added, "But if half the information is true and the other half false it would be a job to figure out what went where."

"You two are smarter than they told me you'd be," Werner said with a grin.

"We do have our moment's sir," Otto said with confidence.

Horst closed his book and tucked into his over coat pocket. It would be safe there from the rains that had tuned to a light mist.

"Sir?" Horst said as he drew his hand out. "I don't want to know where you were or what you did, but is there any way for us to know how to reach you when you're gone?"

Werner crossed his arms and started to waver in his chair. The question wasn't meant to pry but to reassure. In fact, it was flattering in a way that the two Germans cared enough to want to make sure the body was returned to the proper owners, if they ever found it.

"I can't tell you who I work for, only that the magazine is a sponsor," Werner began.

"Oh Christ," Horst said.

Horst and Otto knew the meaning of the term sponsor. It was what was called a second decoy for an operation the CIA usually conducted. An agent may have several sponsors to make sure his tracks are covered and didn't lead back to the original source. It also meant that anyone who worked for the sponsor could easily be tossed in prison as an accomplice, even the man who changed light bulbs in the office could be suspect.

Horst pursued the issue, "When you're gone your gone, but if you don't come back what about us?"

"It's what you get paid for isn't it?" Werner joked.

"Not me, I get paid for taking pictures."

"Horst is right," Otto interjected. "Isn't there something we can look for to let us know in advance? I mean we could be sitting here and then be arrested by the Gray Mice in the blink of an eye."

Werner hesitated and he could see the dilemma the two were in. Then there was the question of loyalty. Would the two Germans be more helpful in the future if he should trust them more now? But if he did tell them everything he ran the risk of widening the scope of too many people knowing too much.

"It's about money," Werner finally said.

"Isn't everything?" Horst said jokingly.

"Wait," Otto said to his friend as he realized Werner was going to include them up to a point.

"UNESCO makes loans to other countries, but makes twice as many grants," Werner began. "Say they make a loan to build a school in Venezuela. Somewhere out in the mountains where nobody goes to see the building being built. And year after year they keep getting grants to build other schools. But instead of using that money they loan it out to Communist countries at a high interest rate?"

"Doesn't anyone at UNESCO check to see if the schools are being built?" Horst asked.

"Of course not, it is the responsibility of Economic Development to see to that and they will never go into the mountains because the rebels would take them hostage and hold them for ransom."

"What about the government auditor of this country?"

"He's usually in on it and keeps two sets of books. Nearly every government official is getting a kick back."

"So just stop sending them the damn money?"

"Based on what, there isn't any proof."

Otto took his copy of the book and slowly slid it inside his coat pocket.

"I think there is now," Otto said.

"Not enough, so wait," Werner added and then left the two to finish their drinks.

CHAPTER 3

"I can't see anything," Sergeant Pogozinski said to the Urlink who was standing beside him, and kneeling at the back of the one thousand pound dud.

The bomb had travelled into the basement of the Headquarters for Military Forces building in the Citadel. It had gone through a concrete wall causing most of the rubble to land on top of it. The war head which housed the laser guidance system was bent to the left and the forward control fins had been ripped off completely. The outer casing had many long groves in the steel and paint looked like it had been sanded off.

"I think there is a small copper door or plate just behind the fins," Urlink said softly as if the bomb would go off if he spoke too loud.

"The fins are gone and I don't see anything like that."

"Should we roll it over it might be on the bottom?"

"Are you crazy?" Pogo shouted, his voice seemed to echo for a short ways.

"The head has to be attached to the fuse and if we move it, it could go off," Pogo added as he straightened up.

"Comrade Sergeant, should I set up the radio recorder back at the truck?" Private Grunn asked.

Pogo gave his Private a sneer, but knew it was probably better than having three dead men to start the first ordnance disposal mission. "Yes, leave one walkie talkie and get the recorders set. Call us when it's ready."

"Yes sergeant," the Private said, snapped a salute and ran for the door. He paused and said, "God be with you Sergeant." then disappeared.

"God doesn't have a damn thing to do with this," Pogo muttered.

"Unless he was the bastard who designed it," Urlink added.

Pogo looked over at the tall Czech with white blonde hair. His face had worn youth written all over it. He was only nineteen but the lack of nourishment throughout his life made him appear as if he was on deaths door.

"Are you with God Urlink?"

"Is that the subject at hand Comrade Sergeant?"

"If I screw this up, it will be the last subject to talk about."

"Then I suggest we wait to see how badly your hand shakes."

"You're correct, let's see if we can get some of this shit off the damn thing," Pogo said and the two set to work carefully clearing the debris away.

The two men worked for a few minutes like archeologists who found a new dig. With slight strokes they brushed dirt and rock from around most of the front part of the bomb to expose the laser guidance warhead. The glass nose cone was shattered and the parts inside had been broken beyond identification. There was no way to determine which part had been connected to the other. Wires of the same color hung out like the tentacles of a small squid.

Suddenly a voice boomed out, "Comrade Sergeant! Can you hear me?"

"Christ!" Pogo yelled and reached for the volume control on the small hand held radio that was resting on a nearby shelf.

Snatching it he made the adjustment and responded. He then handed it to Urlink saying, "You're the relay man."

Urlink took the radio and readjusted the control so there was just a faint sound of static crackling away.

Pogo stood directly over the bomb as if he was going to ride it into town like a motorbike. It then became clear that they needed more light.

The room was mostly dark because it was a place where readers of files usually did their work, but the overhead lighting had been busted out from flying debris as the bomb crashed inside. What was left of a large desk or table was slammed against the back wall and looked like it had been put there deliberately. If there were any chairs, the bits of broken sticks where the only indication they once existed.

"We should go and get the work lights and tool kit," Urlink said.

"Tak," Pogo replied and the two left making sure nothing would fall while they were gone. A sudden tremble could be just what the bomb fuse was waiting for.

*   *   *

The word about the misbehaved bomb had spread over Hanoi like a hurricane. Not to mention the other six bombing attacks that had hit several wrong targets, like the corner of the market place killing dozens. But a direct hit with a dud bomb on Military Headquarters couldn't be contained even if the North had cut the tongues out of everyone in the city.

This direct act of belligerence by the American aggressors brought out Sergeant Wilkins and his men to fill out the 880 forms. When he heard about Military

Headquarters he thought of the great opportunity to get close to the real threat to peace in the country. Perhaps he thought; something might rub off.

The gate to the citadel was blocked by security police when Wilkins pulled up in the blue pickup. He had the foresight to let Bill, John, and Ed, off on different street corners' advising them to get as many 880's filled out as possible and then walk back to Group 6 and inform Captain La Rouch where he had gone.

"You no go inside," the guard at the gate said. "Dangerous!"

"It's okay I'm supposed to be there," Wilkins replied firmly.

"No, no, turn round," The guard said as he waved his hands indicating a reversal in course.

"Look, I'm with the UN and those American bastards are trying to kill us all."

The guard, a scrawny man who's uniform didn't fit right thought for a moment. He seemed to be encouraged by the Canadians sense of loyalty to the North, and didn't know it was a faint.

"You wait, I get officer," the man replied as several of his comrades hung around the truck like vultures.

The guard went inside the portal of the gate and talked on a portable radio. Wilkins could see the man's head boob up and down then from side to side. For a moment Wilkins thought he was waving off a nest of mosquitoes.

The guard returned and asked, "You have gun?"

"No!"

The guard looked over the door and could see that the Sergeant wasn't wearing a holster around his waist. Then said "You go in now."

Wilkins released the break and pulled the truck forward heading down the long avenue that led to the building. On the pavement were shinny scratches that must have come from the bomb as it skipped along at about 150 mph. Up ahead he could see the red truck the Polish EOD group were driving. There was some activity but from such a distance Wilkins couldn't really tell anything.

It was when Wilkins pulled up beside the red truck that he was suddenly struck by the looks on the men's faces. The privates were scared and depressed at the same time. Typical of those who have been shoved into a position with no hope or chance of survival.

Wilkins climbed out and went over to one of the privates he had seen before. He didn't know his name but sometimes it only takes the recollection of seeing someone before to insure trust.

"Where's the bomb?" Wilkins asked.

The private merely shrugged he didn't understand English.

"Boom Whoosh!"

Private Conneski looked up from gathering the tool box, then nodded toward the open door to the basement.

Wilkins turned and went towards it, but at that moment Pogozinski and Corporal Urlink came through the opening.

Wilkins stood at the top of the short flight of steps leading down as Pogo came up to join him.

"You got yourself a bugger of deal this time eh?"

"Some deal," Pogo replied then motioned for Urlink to carry on with getting the tools and work lights ready.

The two NCO's stood talking to each other, their eyes darting back and forth, not because they were watching, but because they were nervous.

"I didn't know you were an EOD man?"

"I'm not, but KGB has great confidence in me."

"You ever done this before?"

"Nie," The Pol replied with contempt. "New bomb type, I never see before."

"Let's take a look," Wilkins said and started down the stairs.

Pogo reached out and grabbed the Sergeant by the shoulder.

"It can go off any time."

"I've got a report to fill out. Let's go eh?"

Pogo motioned for Urlink to get the equipment and follow them down.

CHAPTER 4

M ajor Tennyson's office was uncharacteristically quiet considering all his men were busy with putting bombing reports together. His office was about security and not reporting, but in emergencies his men usually helped out to get things moving faster. It was imperative that the Americans were informed of the damage they had done. Not only that, it was a regulation and the longer it took to get the paperwork through the less chance there was of the validity to the reports.

In the natural order of diplomacy, the office that handled bombing and damage assessment was the Violation of Sovereign Contravention Department of the ICC. The group office was in the basement of the Canadian Embassy and was manned by those who formulated statistics. The statistically reports were based on the visual damage and compared with the potential of economic damage.

For example, if a market is bombed, usually by accident because dumb bombs are like stones tossed in a lake and they rarely landed where they are intended. The destruction of the market and the deaths of those who are there at the time would be one statistic. The economic part of the equation is where will the people go for food when there isn't any market place. And how many people go hungry as a result.

For those who ponder the reduction of hostilities by virtue of prohibition these figures demonstrate that the North is losing the war. What isn't part of the 880 Forms are the supplies brought in covertly from other allied nations. That information appears on Form 972, Report of Breach in Sanctions.

The 972 form, which hardly ever sees the light of day is sent to a different evaluation department and is only reviewed when a flagrant act is committed. Like an entire ship load of small arms is discovered as it is being unloaded in the North's backyard. This Form can also be nullified in any one of several instances. Like the same load of small arms are loaded onto a ferry boat and then brought into the country. The third party escape clause is for the lawyers to chew on and never find a solution to.

So when Major Tennyson began thinking about new sources of getting information for his rolodex data base, he thought of Captain La Rouch and the event leading up to the contact with the East German, whose name was still a mystery.

The circumstances revolved around two situations, the first being an act of compassion that went astray when La Rouch mailed the letters from Lieutenant Ho Buc to his wife in the South using a diplomatic pouch. The second was the meeting between the East German and the Captain and the announcement of appreciation by another government, but whose?

Glancing at the clock on his book shelf he realized the midmorning visit with Captain La Rouch wouldn't be out of the ordinary. Picking up his inner office phone he rang down for his car and driver.

As the Major road along the avenue he could see the locals were getting their day started. The American fighters had left and for once didn't drop any bombs. There was a tremendous roar as a small flight of jet fighters went over. It startled the occupants and both looked up as if they could see through the steel roof of the car.

"Ours or theirs?" Tennyson asked the driver who was straining to get a good look.

"Can't say sir, but it sounds like theirs. Too damn noisy."

The roar dissipated but was followed up by a rattling sound. It was a crackling that vibrated in the exhaust of the jets engine. Only communist planes had it, it was thought to be the sound of might.

The car turned into the Group 6 compound and Tennyson spotted La Rouch inside the garage. The doors were wide open and the Captain looked to be working on a small black car, a Lada to be exact. The one Pogo had supplied to Wilkins so he could get around town without being stopped by the Gray Mice.

"Captain," the Major said as he stepped from the car and returned a salute.

La Rouch had snapped to attention before the car door was open and gave the customary gesture of respect. "Sir," the Captain replied.

"Keeping the equipment in shape I see."

"Sir!"

Tennyson glanced over the oily engine, he knew of the reliability of Soviet made vehicles and hated having this one around. But necessity was the mother of invention and all good solider never look a gift horse in the mouth.

"Where's your crew?"

"They're all out sir. Sergeant Wilkins took them early this morning after last night's raid. Bound to be a couple of bad one's sir."

"Right, I wouldn't be surprised," Tennyson said as he swung a leg over the fender and took on casual seating.

"At ease Captain," Tennyson said with as warm a grin as he could muster. It wasn't common for him to be in a placid state.

La Rouch stepped to one side to get a better look at the major. He wasn't sure what to expect but if the major came to see him it couldn't be good.

"You know with all this invasion stuff going on down south our sources of information are a bit strained. So I'm thinking of expanding our network as it were."

"I thought that was Bishop and Wilkins job sir?"

"Yes it is, but for those two it seems it's only a small part. Bishop has a time of it."

"Did his trial go well sir?"

"Yes, he's restricted to base so to speak and he forfeits a month's pay. In fact that's why I sent him to Group 5, I was afraid they'd arrest him on the spot and we'd never get him back."

"That bad eh?"

"Well it wasn't so much the problem with the guard, as it was when they came back with that load of wounded. I nice touch for relations but we had some talking to do about why the hell they were out there at the time. We came up with the story they were out making an agricultural delivery. The North didn't buy it, so the next time he gets into trouble he's going to have two loads dumped on him. The original screw up and this story."

"I don't suppose we could make up a better story and claim that the evidence wasn't available until a later date."

Tennyson thought for a moment. There had to be some veracity in what the captain had just proposed.

"That might not be bad idea Captain. I think I'll suggest it to legal and see what they say?"

"Well if it could help sir."

The Major rose and walked around to the passenger side door and looked inside. The interior wasn't in the best of shape, but he had never seen a Lada that was.

"You know that little problem we had with Lieutenant Hoa Buc back last month?"

"Yes sir. I haven't said anything to him about his wife."

"Yes, and that East German, who was he?"

"I don't know sir, he didn't give his name."

"Right, well I think we need to find him."

"That isn't going to be easy sir. It's not like we can look him up in the phone book eh?"

"Right, but I was wondering if you had ever seen this Lieutenant talking with any foreigners when you're on one of those trips to the airport for supplies and mail?"

"No sir, Ho Buc is always alone when I'm there."

"So we don't know this Germans name but we do know he has some kind of contact with the Americans?"

"Yes sir, at least in Wichita Kansas."

"I'm guessing CIA?"

"We're on the same track sir."

"I think I might have a way into that."

"How sir."

"Roth, the Deputy Director asked me to go along with him to Hong Kong on Friday. He's meeting with some Agricultural committee from the North and China. Something about rice production I suppose."

"I wouldn't think he'd need security on that?"

"He doesn't just an out of office work fair for me. But I know someone in the British Consulate there who used to work for MI. He's bound to know something."

"And me sir?"

"I was wondering if you couldn't walk about and keep your eyes open for anything that might be connected to Germany. I think either East or West, no telling which side of the Wall he's from."

"And the Lieutenant. Should I tell him about his wife?"

The Major paused to think. Would Buc be a good communist and turn them in or would he keep his mouth shut? It was the unintended circumstances that were the main consideration. But if Buc's wife is in the US like the German had said; any turning in might get messy.

"I'm going to leave it up to your discretion Captain."

"Thank you sir. I think."

Major smiled and slapped the Captain on the shoulder. "All part of growing up son."

La Rouch also smiled and gave a parting salute which the Major didn't return. But it really didn't matter; La Rouch knew he was gaining ground on the Major's good side.

CHAPTER 5

It looked like a half buried cow; Wilkins thought when he first spotted the dud bomb in the rubble. The basement was dimly lit and the wreckage seemed to have found its own new home. Dust was everywhere because the foundations of the old building were showing signs of age with respect to the masonry that was decaying into powder.

Pogo stepped past Wilkins followed by Urlink carrying a bag of tools from the truck. Dropping the bag beside the bomb Urlink retreated to go after the work lights.

Wilkins took up a post on the left wall about ten feet away. He was close enough to see most everything, yet not impinging on the two EOD men. The Canadian could clearly see the bent nose of the guidance system on the tip of the bomb.

"It's big isn't it?" Wilkins said; his nerves were a bit shaky.

"Well, you know the Americans? It's big enough," Pogo replied as he knelt down beside the nose. He could see the components lying on the floor like broken glass.

"You Canada have EOD?" Pogo asked looking up at the Sergeant

"Not a chance in hell my friend."

"I have book on bombs but it from Moscow and ten years old."

"Did it cover American ordnance?"

"Tak, from World War Two."

Wilkins was starting get his courage back. His mind began to focus like this was just another job, instead of a death defying second guessing exercise. Thinking of all the books and records he had seen at the embassy he didn't recall anything that covered this type of affair.

"You know there is only one man who might be able to help us, and he isn't that far away."

"Who?"

"Corporal Bishop, he used to serve with the Americans, he might have picked up something."

Urlink returned carrying a tripod and bank of hundred watt light bulbs. He placed it in a corner, shoving wood aside so the legs could sit even on the concrete floor. He managed to find a socket and plugged in. The room was so bright the others had to shield their eyes. It was like looking into the sun and the room was beginning to warm up.

"I'll have to get in touch with our embassy."

"Good, you have radio?"

"No, I'll have to find a phone."

"We have radio in truck, Private Grunn help you."

"I'll be right back," Wilkins replied and slipped up stairs.

Pogo looked over at Urlink. It was that kind of look that was more of an unspoken question than a statement.

*   *   *

Private Grunn was a young man of good stature. His bark brown hair was longer than regulation and stuck up from under his red beret like eagle wings. He had a long face that was marked by a mild case of acne, but his gray eyes seemed to look right through a man. Something soldiers get after a long deployment.

Wilkins told him what he wanted and surprisingly Grunn was able to understand. To Wilkins it seemed almost intuitive for the Pol. The radio was a large box with a whip antenna bolted to the back of the cab on the truck. There was a short white ribbon tied to the end of it, a type of flag so they could see it from a distance even when the rest of the truck was blocked from view.

Wilkins adjusted the dials slightly and made his call.

The operator at the embassy was Sergeant Grondon who was a wizard at communications. Amelia Earhart would have never gone missing if Grondon was on the key that night.

"Ottawa base this is Wilkins calling over."

"Got you strength nine Wilkins, what's going on eh?"

"Look Bill, I'm over here at the Citadel with the Polish Brigade. I need you to get me in touch with group 5."

"No problem, I was just talking to them, daily reports and stuff."

"Right. Gettum' back I need to talk with Bishop."

"Is he in trouble again?"

"No, just get him and set up a relay link if you can. I'm on the Pol's radio frequency 014.2."

"Hold on Wilkins I'll put it on scrambler."

As the call was made Wilkins glanced about the cargo box of the red truck. It was kitted out in proper fashion for a WARSAW Pac country. Shovels, hammers, two types of drills, electric and hand crank, lengths of climbing rope and canvas bags of tools.

Kirk, the wireless operator on the Vergil had finished sending his daily report to the embassy and not wanting to join the others' who were engaged in putting up walls for Bishops new NCO quarters, was looking through a copy of Time magazine from two years earlier.

"Group 5, this is Ottawa Base over."

Kirk grabbed the receiver with a sweeping hand and replied.

"What did I forget this time?"

"Nothing, Wilkins wants to talk with the Canadian Yankee."

Kirk put down the receiver that was more like an office phone and went up on deck. From there he could yell to the barracks where Bishop and Mike were working on putting up a wall partition.

"Hey Corp, its Wilkins for you!"

"What the fuck does he want?" Bishop said as banged in a nail to hold the wall in place.

Giving his tool to Mike to finish the job Bishop went to the boat at the end of the pier. Climbing up onto the bridge he reached through the door as Kirk handed him the phone.

"What's our call sign?"

Kirk was confused and then replied, "Its NATO 5."

"Okay this is NATO 5 to. What's his call sign?" Bishop asked.

"Doesn't have one Corp, this like a phone line."

"Oh!" Bishop said and the confusion was over. "Hey Sarge what's happnin'?"

"Got a problem at this end Bishop, I think you can help."

"Lay it on me my man."

"You remember Pogo?"

"Yea your Polish sergeant buddy. I got it"

"Well he's now a bomb disposal unit and we're sitting on one of those Laser jobs, you know the ones."

"I hope you mean it's a dud?"

"We aren't really sure at this point," Wilkins replied nervously.

"You got to be shitten' me Ralph. Where is it?"

"It's in the basement of the North's Military Headquarters building."

"Say what?"

"Yea!"

"I got an idea," Bishop joked. "Get the fuck out of there and let the thing blow up. Tell the dinks you did your best."

"Can't do that."

Bishop put his hand over the receiver and muttered to Kirk who was listening in on a head set. "Of course you can't you honest son of bitch." Taking his hand away he added, "So why not?"

"Come on Corporal, you know why."

"Okay so what do you want me to do?"

"We thought you might know how to defuse the thing. Nobody around here has any info on it. The book Pogo's got on ordnance only goes back to the 1940's."

"Oh fuck sarge get out of there will yea?"

"Are you going to help us or no?"

Bishop paused to think. He had to break things down into smaller bits to put it together. A puzzle is best realized when all the parts are spread out, rather than bunched up.

"Okay, it's an air force type right, it came from a bomber?"

"No, it's from a fighter attack plane I think."

"Then it's a Navy jet and it must be off one of the carriers out here."

"The damn guidance part of the bomb is bent all to hell, we have no idea how to get to the detonator," Wilkins commented.

It seemed he was farther ahead with estimating than Bishop was. The Corporal could tell Wilkins was in over his head by the way his sentences were two thoughts before the question.

"Okay sarge, hold on a minute I need some head time." Bishop replied as he let the receiver dangle between his fingers.

Kirk was looking up at Bishop from his chair in the radio room. He was only a few feet away and it seemed they could feel each other's breath on their faces. For a moment Kirk's confidence in the Corporal was starting to wane, but then the situation was so unique he wondered if anyone could figure it out.

Looking straight at Kirk Bishop asked, "Okay so if the planes from a carrier how do we get in touch with them?"

"No problem Corp," Kirk replied as he reached around and yanked a red binder off a shelf.

Flipping open the book he ran his finger down the index and found the call sign for the USS Forrestal, an aircraft carrier that was part of the US Navy's battle group that was laying a hundred miles off the North's shore and in international waters. Turning to the corresponding page number Kirk found the frequency and call sign.

But before Kirk could make the connection Bishop spotted something on the page that was very curious.

"Hold on a minute," Bishop said as he reached down and stuck a finger on one of the entries. "Is that listing of 'FAC' mean forward air controller?"

"Yup," Kirk replied casually, his hand holding the dial on his radio set. "They swim into shore now and then."

"You mean we got SEAL's running strike missions in Hai Phong?"

"Is that a surprise?"

"No," Bishop replied in contempt. "That's not a surprise."

Kirk adjusted the settings and handed another receiver to the Corporal who was starting to look like he was being wired into the communications equipment.

Kirk pointed to the entry on the page. "Here's the call sign. Red Deer 73."

"Red Deer 73 this is NATO 5 over."

"NATO 5 go?" came a firm voice, the kind that was overly assured of their competence.

"I need to talk to your armaments officer?"

"Who is this again," the young voice queried.

"Its NATO 5 dip shit now get me the man!" Bishop yelled, for a moment Bishop was in one of his bad places, reflections of calling in artillery on his on position from a past experience washed over him like a wave of cold water.

"Wait one over."

A second passed and another voice, this one more mature asked, "This is Commander Parker I'm the communications officer."

"I don't want you sir, I want the ordnance officer!"

"What for?"

"We've got a thousand pounder down here and it's a dud. How do we disarm it?"

"Wait one," came the reply.

The responding voice had the kind of tone in it that didn't exhume confidence but more like being sucked into the endless system of questions and answers to the point Bishop would just hang up.

"You say you're with NATO?" a different voice asked, his tone was raspy like a bartender who enjoyed his job.

"Who the fucks this and yea?" Bishop called back.

"You the Canadian Yankee, name of Bishop?" the voice asked without identifying itself.

"Give me a break will ya sir, we got a serious problem here," Bishop replied almost in a begging tone.

"Wait one!"

"Oh for fuck sakes," Bishop said as he lowered his receiver.

"How do they know you Corp?" Kirk asked curiously.

"Hey, with my personality how can you forget me?"

"I know I won't Corp." Kirk said.

"This is Admiral Wakefield, Bishop."

Bishop eyes grew wide at the thoughts of being kicked upstairs to the boss's office as it were.

"Yes sir admiral!"

"Our armaments man is on his way up. Are you at the bomb site?"

"No sir, I'm the relay man."

"Okay, what we will try to do is help you as much as possible, but you have to understand this is highly classified information," the admiral said, his voice was like steel in a vice.

"Yes sir, but you have to understand there's a bunch of people whose lives depend on this. Those fucking duds are everywhere now."

Bishop exaggerated his point, he didn't know of any others but merely assumed this couldn't be the only one after weeks of bombing raids over Hanoi. And for a moment he was beginning to believe that this was more about people and not targets.

"You do know that this typically goes through channels and the diplomatic corps?"

"Yes sir, but we need to get the job done now, not wait for the eagle to shit sir."

"I understand, but I have a boss too."

"Yes sir. And I hope he's an understanding man sir."

"Good luck Bishop!"

"Thank you sir," the Corporal replied as the static took over the airwaves.

All Bishop could do now was to wait for the officer that would help out, if he was willing enough.

CHAPTER 6

It was Sergeant Grondon at the embassy communication room that thought of it. He had been listening in on the back and forth conversations and he was fully aware of the situation. The question suddenly dawned on him what would happen if there was a mistake and the whole thing went up in smoke.

With the various team members involved, and once everyone was together going over what had happened and what caused the disaster, and with the various countries protecting what they knew by lying, who was going to provide the actual facts up to the point of termination? That could only happen if someone was to record the entire problem from front to back.

Grondon reached over and threw a couple switches which started the two big wheels of recording tape to turn slowly. There was over five hours of recording time left.

"NATO 5 this is Red Deer over."

Bishop sat up and keyed his receiver. "Go ahead Red Deer."

"Okay, I'm commander Holcomb ordnance officer of the Forrestal, who's your point man."

"Its Sergeant Wilkins sir, he's at the bomb site."

"Sergeant Wilkins come in over."

"Hold on sir I gotta' tune you in," Bishop replied and made the correct changes for the communications to be direct.

"You're coming in at seven strength sir," Wilkins said as coolly as he could muster.

"Okay Wilkins what's the condition of the bomb?"

"Its half buried in wall sir and the warhead is bent 90 degrees. The front fins are gone and some wires are hanging out of the nose."

"Okay take some electrical tape and wrap the ends of the wires."

Pogo was the one who asked why and Wilkins past it on. "Why is that sir?"

"When the bomb leaves the ship we prime the electric boosters and the charge lasts 23 hours. Those wires are connected to the primer and detonator. Any static electricity can set off the bomb, if a plane flies over and keys the mike it could set the bomb off."

"Static electricity?" Wilkins said sheepishly.

"Yea, so make sure those wires are wrapped."

"Ah sir," Wilkins began in a low voice making sure Pogo couldn't hear him. "I'm on a walkie talkie."

"Damn sergeant, get the hell out of there and put in a land line. Get at least five hundred yards away," Holcomb ordered.

"I'll call you back when I'm set up sir," Wilkins replied nervously.

"Okay Sergeant."

Suddenly there's an increase in static sounds as Wilkins turned off his radio. It was nothing to worry about all radios do the same thing when switched off.

"Bishop are you there?"

"Yes sir, just holdin' my own," he replied as he leaned back in his chair.

"Where the hell is this damn bomb anyway?"

"It's in the basement of the North's military headquarters."

"Damn son I thought it was in a hospital or something."

"Hospital headquarters what's the difference sir?"

"The difference is that's a legitimate target and a hospital isn't."

"There still people sir."

"They're the enemy Bishop."

"I believe the Constitution protects people sir."

"It doesn't cover the enemy."

"Well if it didn't sir, then we wouldn't have any of their POW's right?"

"You're twisting the words Corporal."

"No sir, those words were twisted long before I did it."

"I got to go to the head mister, I'll be back shortly."

"I'll be here sir."

Bishop leaned back and his chair and it struck the hull of the boat with a thud. In the cramped space it was hard to tell which way the sound came from.

"You think he'll be back Corp?" Kirk asked; he was squatting down to keep his head close to the speaker.

"I hope so," Bishop replied. "For Wilkins sake if nothing else."

CHAPTER 7

"Bishop, are you there?" came Wilkins voice over the receiver.

Bishop who had taken over Kirks chair in the radio room of the Vergil nearly fell onto the deck. He straightened himself and pulled the microphone which was lying on the desk to his mouth. Kirk was standing on the bridge and he stuck his head inside so he could hear better.

"Yea buddy, you got your shit together yet?"

"Yes, we set up a land line down to Pogo and he's on the other end with a head set. I think his mate Urlink is helping out."

"Good having two guys is better than one in a situation like this," Bishop contended.

"It also means one extra dead if we don't do this right."

"War is hell as they say!"

Bishop was about to reach for one of the phones that was clipped into a special relay device. There were two phones present; one went to the Forrestal the other to the embassy. Through special wiring it was like the two lines were connected at the hip as it were. A small speaker allowed Bishop to hear the conversations and the microphone gave him the chance to intervene in the conversation if necessary.

"I'm calling our buddies out at sea," Bishop said and then through the interrupt switch.

This allowed Bishop to talk directly to Commander Holcomb, but Wilkins couldn't overhear them. He made his appeal to the ordnance officer who came back nearly instantly.

"This is commander Holcomb, over."

"I guess were still in business sir. No extra holes in the foundation yet."

"Okay Bishop, am I through to Wilkins?"

Bishop reset the interrupt switch and replied, "You are now sir."

"Go ahead sir, read you seven strength," Wilkins replied.

"Okay Wilkins, what's your situation?"

Wilkins informed Holcomb of the communications hook up and where Pogo was. Wilkins was running the relay from the radio to the land line and he could hear Pogo's heavy breathing from the other end. Wilkins could tell it was getting hotter down inside the basement by the way Pogo's breathing increased when the tricky stuff needed to be done.

"First things first," Holcomb said. "For future reference you need to cover the bomb with some kind of reflective material. Something that won't let electronic signals penetrate, like a radar cover or something. Make it like a tent so you can work under it."

"Right sir, I think we can handle that," Wilkins said confidently.

"That reminds me wait one."

This sudden stop in the conversation of instructions became worry some both to Bishop and Wilkins. The radio crackled with static and it left both men thinking they might have done something wrong. Something left out; a piece of detail unreported could make for a catastrophic incident.

As the Canadians waited for the return of the expert, Holcomb was talking to others on board the ship. The Commander suddenly realized that his previous statement of keying a mike from a passing plane might set off the bomb accidently had to be addressed before the conversation could continue.

Taking up a different receiver Holcomb called the bridge of his ship. "Holcomb to Skycap."

"Air ops. Go ahead sir," A voice replied.

"Tell air ops I want a red flag over Hanoi for the next hour."

"I think they're getting ready to launch a strike sir."

"I don't give a damn, get the no fly up!"

"Yes sir," the sailor answered somewhat reluctantly.

"Okay Sergeant I'm back," Holcomb reported.

There was a collective sigh of relief at the sound of the Commanders voice but the Navy thought it was some kind of interference.

Wilkins was first to speak, "Just thought I'd tell you sir the Pol's have built a lovely canopy of corrugated sheet metal over the bomb sir." Wilkins thought this new information would make points with the Navy. They were showing their prowess at dealing with the situation in a productive way.

"A steel roof, Sergeant all they've done is built an antenna over the thing. Get it down!"

"Yes sir, but the boys did do a great job."

"I don't care Sergeant get the damn thing down."

"It's going to take some doing sir, if we can just get on with the bomb?"

Holcomb became frustrated. He was trying to help and he was becoming overwhelmed by the naiveté of the men who had never disarmed a bomb before. To him it was routine but explaining such work to novices was taking its toll.

Finally he called back, "I don't know why I should bother; you clowns are going to kill yourselves even with my help."

"Sir, we're ready here?" Wilkins said; he was trying to keep the American focused and to overlook things that hadn't caused problems yet. All the information was very useful, and taking out the stupid bits later was much more advantageous.

"Okay Wilkins," Holcomb replied somewhat less angrily. "Are the tail fins on the bomb exposed?"

There was a pause as Wilkins asked Pogo the question and the answer came back almost instantly. This part of the relay was working better than the radio.

"Yes sir."

"Good. Where the fins are attached to the casing there's a little red button in the middle of the fins. Use a screw driver and press that in."

"Done sir."

"Okay, turn the fins clockwise."

This order took a few moments to get a reply because Urlink had to position himself to turn the fins while Pogo held down the button.

"Right sir, fins are turning."

"Take them all the way off."

"Right sir."

When Urlink finished the final twist the fins fell into his lap like a cannon ball out of its barrel. The two Pol's could see a red bolt the size of a baseball in the end of the bomb.

"Okay turn that bolt clockwise it should drop out after a half turn."

"It did sir."

"Okay now look inside you see the Irish mushroom?"

"The what sir," Wilkins called back slightly confused.

"It's a bright green circular ball with a pin sticking out of the top."

"Right, we see it."

"Use needle nose players and pull that ball out by the pin. There's a nine inch shaft connected to the end of the ball. When it's out it looks like a green mushroom."

"Got it sir."

"Okay, the bombs primary fuse is disengaged so we don't have to worry about electricity anymore."

"Outa sight sir!" Bishop yelled into his receiver.

"We're not done yet mister Bishop."

"Sorry sir," Bishop said and leaned back in his chair.

It was then the Corporal looked up at Kirk and the others who had joined them. The entire Group was present and mystified by the doings.

"Okay Wilkins, "Holcomb said. "Now roll the bomb over and at the nose where the guidance system connects there is a small hatch type door with a slot in it for a screw driver."

At the bomb site there was some jubilance as Wilkins called for more restraint. "We found it sir," Wilkins finally answered.

"Okay, put a slot screw driver in it and turn counter clock wise a quarter turn. It should fall out or pop open."

There was a longer pause in the communications. Wilkins could hear Pogo and Urlink struggling with the weight of the bomb. It was like trying to move a truck with its parking brake on, but because of the rounded edges the bomb could be fulcrummed into place.

"Right sir, got it," Wilkins reported, the delay was beginning to raise tensions again, but it quickly dissipated.

"Okay, use needle nose players and pull that white circuit board out."

"Should we watch about not touching the sides of the bomb and making contact?"

"No, the circuit board is just a fuse switch that connects the charge to the detonator."

"Right sir, its out."

"Okay you can start breathing again the bombs completely disarmed," Holcomb said with relief.

There's the sound of howling and screaming of joy over the set as Holcomb began smiling. On the Forrestal those involved began glad handing and shoulder slapping.

"That wasn't so bad sir," Bishop cut in as he hit the interrupt switch.

"We've got three minutes to rearm a bird; we have to make it easy for the deck crews," Holcomb replied.

"I buy that sir."

"Now a word of caution mister Bishop," Holcomb said firmly. "These are Navy ordnance; the air force may be different. And everything I told you today may not work a couple months from now. They're developing these things as we speak and the changes are pulling our hair out."

"You got it sir."

"And another thing."

"Yes sir?"

"Next time, call somebody else."

"I love you too sir," Bishop replied with a grin.

*   *   *

From his chair on the bride of the Forrestal the Admiral could survey the gray horizon and listen to the steam catapults flinging fighters from his ship like clay pigeons. The seas were choppy but not a threat to pilots returning from their missions.

There was little to be serene about, but the Admiral always took time to review happenings about the ship. From who dropped a can of shoe polish on the deck to what type of bombs were to be dropped this time around. His concentration was broken when he heard Holcomb's voice behind him.

"Permission to speak sir?"

The Admiral nodded but didn't turn to face the young Commander.

"How did it go?"

"There still alive sir, and we'll probably have to drop another one down their throats next week," Holcomb replied, as he kept to the side of the Admiral rather than speak face on.

"Use regular bombs not this smart stuff for a while."

"Yes sir, which brings me to why I wanted to see you."

"Yes Commander?"

"I wouldn't be surprised if every damn commie for a thousand miles didn't listen in to our conversation."

"Well I wouldn't worry about it too much Commander."

"Why not Admiral?"

"Time of day Commander. The North is listening to our pilots so they know which way we're coming from. And secondly, the conversations were on International Maritime scramblers. Only the fishermen ever listen to those channels."

"But it was classified information, can I get into trouble?"

"Not you mister. Me!" The Admiral explained.

"What can we expect sir?"

"Oh the usual," the Admiral said as he shifted in his chair. As comfortable as they were; the Admiral's chair always felt a little over stuffed. "They'll say I was out of my mind. Dereliction of duty, etcetera, etcetera"

"I've been reading the test results on these new LGB's and the dud rate is climbing. Even the air force is worried," Holcomb said in a form of justification.

"I'm wondering if we aren't dropping from too low an altitude," The Admiral speculated. "The scanner doesn't have time to find the beam, and not only that we're discovering the damn things aren't any good in smoke or bad weather."

"Then I guess all we've done is piss off the diplomats?"

"Your right, Commander. Someone in Washington was going hold the EOD information up as a bargaining chip to get the North back to the peace table, and now we've taken that away."

"I think Bishop might have said it sir in a roundabout way."

"What?" the Admiral said as he glanced over at Holcomb.

"We high tech barbarians need to show some compassion every now and then. It might help somewhere along the line."

"I hope he's right." The Admiral replied.

In a philosophical way, Bishop was making a point. It may be necessary for those who carry a big stick to know when to use it, and when to put it down.

CHAPTER 8

A scientist once put a cat in a box with a vile of poison. The poison was in a container that slowly dissolved and would eventually expose the cat to toxic fumes killing the animal. It was deduced that the cat was neither alive nor dead. The supposition was that there was no way to know the condition of the cat until you opened the box.

For Sergeant Wilkins who had gathered his flock of report makers and deposited them back at Group 6 before going on to the embassy to see the major, he was feeling a little like the cat. Not really knowing if he was alive or dead, philosophically speaking.

Wilkins and Pogo had done something that was nearly impossible and would have been if Bishop hadn't pulled another miracle out of his butt.

For Pogo, he moved on to the next dud, knowing he had the information to do the job without loss of his life and others. So for him there was closure. But for Wilkins, he merely went on his way as if he had just witnessed an accident on the freeway while driving to work.

This feeling is one of the dispositions of combat veterans. Even though Wilkins career had provided him with a lot of shooting opportunities, just the fact they lived to tell of it wasn't enough. Survival of a dramatic situation is more often than not to be accompanied by the remorseful feeling of living through it. It's jubilation and tragedy all at the same time. What lasts beyond the moment into later life is usually guilt.

With the French in Algeria, eventually a peace was signed and Algeria gained its independence, so there was closure even in the sense the French lost the colony, those who lived became their own nation. And that transfer of authority was monumental enough for all to appreciate the sacrifices. Henceforth; providing closure.

But Vietnam was different. There didn't seem to be an end, or even a stalemate like Korea. And with the Easter invasion, it just seemed like another exercise in futility. After all, the North had been at war for over 60 years in one form or another.

And those were the momentary contemplations he had as Wilkins turned into the embassy courtyard and parked his truck. Switching off the engine seemed to coincide with the dispensing of emotional evaluation as he climbed out and headed for the Major's office.

"Well Sergeant, seems you're a national hero around here," Tennyson said as he met Wilkins in the hallway not far from the office.

Wilkins smiled and tucked his beret under his belt as the two walked briskly to the confines of the Majors workplace. Neither said anything but the Major reached for the door knob first and ushered Wilkins in as if he was the Consulate General.

"Sir," Wilkins began as Tennyson seated himself behind his desk. "I thought you might want to talk to me about our little incident out there."

"Of course Sergeant, take a seat," Tennyson replied as he motioned for Wilkins to relax a bit in a comfortable chair.

"From what we all heard out there on the radio you did a bang up job and have brought great credit to our embassy. We may even get a seal from Ottawa on this one."

What the major was referring to was that whenever members of a Consulate did some extraordinary act Ottawa would issue a small plaque with the Canadian Seal on it as a reward and acknowledgement for work well done. It wasn't handed out generously.

"This'll show McCollum that we aren't the back seat boys he thinks we are." Tennyson said boastingly.

The Major didn't like the Ambassador much because of his indifference to all issues at hand. The lack of making decisions was of a paralyzing nature and that couldn't stand with the military.

"I'm putting you in for a rank advancement. You've earned it!"

"Thank you sir, but Bishop was also a part of this."

"Ah Bishop," Tennyson said as he swung around in his chair and faced the wall to his right. "Now there's an anomaly, and I thank God for him sometimes."

"He dose deserve some recognition on this one sir."

"Not a snowballs chance in hell Sergeant. Our little asset is getting to be too well known in these parts."

"But sir the things he's done to help us and others."

"Yes, and what about his little backside flaunts," Tennyson said still looking at the blanch wall as if Bishops whole life were written on it. "I had to send him to Group 5 to keep him from being tossed into jail for that accident with the rock.

And now yesterday Captain Scott tells me he almost executed the Captain on one of the North's patrol boats."

"I didn't know about the boating problem."

"Oh course you don't," Tennyson said as he swung back around to face the NCO. "How would it look if we pin a medal on him for arranging this dud bomb stuff and then have the North issue a citation for attempted execution of one of their officers?"

Wilkins eyes dropped to the floor, he was feeling somewhat reluctant to pursue Bishop's recognition for bravery. "I understand how you feel sir. There was an incident when we were getting the POW's out."

"Oh!"

"Yes sir, I left it out of my report, but I had to draw my weapon on him. He wanted to take the POW's all the way to the extraction point which was in Laos. I couldn't let him cross the border unauthorized. I mean how would he get back if he was captured?"

"Probably step into a phone booth, put on his red cape and fly back I suppose," Tennyson said frustratingly. "You did do the right thing Sergeant. And thanks for telling me that."

"Sir, isn't there anything we can do?"

"My hands are tied Sergeant. Surly you see that. The man goes out and dose something wonderful then shoots his foot off. How can I put him up for anything?"

"Yes sir, I understand."

"There is one thing I might try."

"Yes sir," Wilkins replied; he suddenly became hopeful for his friend.

"I'm going to see if we can get more lawyers in on this."

Wilkins smiled and shook his head. Bishop was a problem, and there didn't seem to be a cure.

Rising, the sergeant left the office and thought a warm glass of tea might help in the café across the street.

*   *   *

Mia had just finished her tour at the hospital, she was tired. Her promotion from bed pan washer to lead nurse in emergency might have looked nice on her resume' but it took its toll on her physically. She looked older than her twenty six years, and much sadder.

The café was self-sustaining in regards to the staff. They had worked for her for more than two years and were as reliable as clock work. One of the staff was with her the night they used the laser bomb targeting device on the freight house, and he was more dependable than anyone she knew. Now with her long hours at the hospital all she could do is sit and relax, and try to forget all the suffering faces of the locals.

As an added insult to suffering, the monsoon rains had turned in another drenching and the streets were nearly empty. Mia took a sip of tea and looked out the opening in the shop. She could see a figure come out of the Canadian Embassy across the street and she recognized Wilkins by his stature.

Mia forced a friendly smile as the Sergeant came running in trying to stay as dry as possible. In monsoon once your wet its forever.

"Hello Mai, can I join you" Wilkins asked, a few drops of water fell from the leading edge of his beret and landed on the table like tears.

She motioned for him to sit and he complied. Raising his hand to attract the women behind the counter he managed to get a glass of hot tea delivered rather quickly.

"I haven't seen you in a while and just wanted to say hello eh?"

"Yes, it is good to see you," she replied and held out her hand. Wilkins gently grasped it in a warm hand shake. The kind you would give Mrs. Trudeau if you ever were that close.

Wilkins held the grasp for a moment, something felt good to him and he didn't want to give it up that easily. The day's events were beginning to tumble into a vote of confidence that might prove interesting.

Mai gently pulled her hand free and took a strong grip on her glass. She could sense Wilkins was drawing closer, and she wasn't sure if it was right at that moment.

"Look, I was wondering if you'd be able to join me for dinner tonight eh?"

"I work tonight at the hospital."

"What time do you need to be there?"

"Midnight."

"Not a problem eh, I'll have you back in plenty of time for that."

"I would have to go home and change you see; and I don't have ride to get there."

"That too isn't a problem, my trucks across the street."

"I don't know," she said softly. It had been year's since she was out with a man. It was when she was in Edmonton at the University that she had suitors, not many but a few. "I can't be late for work yes?"

"Let me go get the truck, I'll drop you off and pick you up later." Wilkins was nearly falling over himself with the possibility of having someone besides three Privates and a Captain for dinner guests.

Mai hesitated, not wanting to give the man any more confidence than he already had. But a date was something she hadn't enjoyed for a while and just the kind of break from the war she needed to boost her spirits.

CHAPTER 9

For a few hours the sun came out after lunch. It was warm and felt good but the air was still damp and cool. To the west the edges of the storm clouds were being licked by silvery light and the definition of rain was absent.

The Vergil swayed at her moorings as the wake of other vessels rambled past. Kirk maintained his post in the radio room; it was almost a permanent position because he was the only operator who knew how to get the equipment to function properly. And whenever the embassy called he was ready to receive.

Bishop and Mike, after being released from dud disposal and the round of congratulatory declarations had gone back to finish the room they were building. An NCO, as Bishop put it, should be separated from the help. Visions of his black lighted hooch back at Camp Eagle in South Vietnam flowed through his mind and it was the best retreat any grunt could have. His only problem was; where was he going to get posters of Credence Clearwater to hang on his walls.

It was perfect timing Mike thought, when Greg turned the corner with three bottles of Molson's Ale in his hand. The alcohol was imported via Air Canada and the usual dispatches brought along for the ride. There was never enough so rationing was a priority.

"Hey Bruekies!" Bishop said and tossed down his hammer.

"Some people call it that," Greg said as he handed one of the bottles to the Corporal.

But upon closure inspection Bishop noticed the bottles, although looked right, had no labels on them.

"What do you call it?" Bishop asked holding the bottle up to the light to see if there was anything in the container that shouldn't be.

"Donkey Dong," Greg said as he took a swig.

"Donkey Dong?" Bishop said rather surprised.

"Yea," Mike added. "If you've ever had oral sex with a donkey that's what it would taste like."

"Are you speaking from experience?" Bishop queried.

"Right, it's supposed to be a party eh," Mike added

Bishop assumed this was part of the initiation of new guys and joined in by taking a huge swallow. When the actual flavor hit his palate he spit it out like it was poisoned.

"Holy shit, you Canadians are something else yea know that?"

The three sailors were laughing so hard they nearly gave up some of their own drinks.

"Between you guys and those clowns at Group 6 and their cabbage wine, you guys should be arrested."

"He's more Yankee than Canadian eh," Mike teased.

"He's been living the good life in the states, can't handle a little tough job eh."

"Come on Corp, drink up!" Mike said and the three made another go of it.

The bottles were nearly empty when Bishop commented, "This shit ain't to bad yea know?"

"Told ya," Greg said laughingly.

It was then Captain Scott entered the room holding onto a clipboard with a stack of reports on it. The men tried to hide their drinks by slipping the bottles behind them.

"Never mind that," Scott said because he was aware of the liquid break. "How's it coming Corporal?"

"As you can see sir, were getten' there."

"Right, have you any clean fatigues?"

"Not right now sir, I only have two sets and the others aren't clean."

"Right, Mike get the Vergil cranked up and take the Corporal here over to the laundry."

"What's up sir?" Bishop asked while putting his bottle down on the bench beside him.

"The Major's coming down to see you tomorrow in the afternoon. He's got some agricultural tattoo to be at then he's coming here."

"To see me huh?"

"Yes, he was supposed to be here today but the equipment broke down so they put it off till tomorrow."

"Okay sir."

"Oh," Scott said as he turned to leave. "Get this place tidied up a bit he'll be in his inspection mode when he gets here."

"You got it sir," Bishop replied and then glanced at the others as if to pass on the order visually.

*   *   *

Sergeant Wilkins hadn't felt so happy about the littlest things in years. With all of his duties that never seemed to have a conclusion he had forgotten what it was like to be on a date. Especially with a beautiful young woman.

After changing into his civilian clothes he went directly to the garage and started digging the Lada out from under its covers. He had dropped Mai off near her house, but not at it. The suspicion of a young woman soldier being deposited at her door in a blue UN vehicle could arouse even the least curious. And so on the way back to Group 6 he thought if he were to pick her up in a Polish embassy car that would at least keep the neighbors confused.

Once the covers were off Wilkins climbed in and tried the starter and of course it didn't fire up. So he climbed out, being careful to not get grease on his clothes and gave the engine a good hard whack with a hammer and tried it again. And like magic, the car sputtered to life enough to get it lose from its hiding place.

Wilkins climbed out and stuck the small Polish flag in the center of the hood where it was supposed to go and reseated himself behind the wheel. Just as he was about to pull out into the street Captain La Rouch curved in through the gate, nearly hitting a large rock by the wall.

Wilkins paused, he saw the Captain flag him to wait. The Lada threatened to take a long nap, but Wilkins goosed it a couple times to remind it; they were on a very important mission.

"Glad I caught you Sergeant," La Rouch said as he walked up to the driver side window which was down.

"Yes sir, the Major wants me to check out a new contact sir. Thought I'd take a run over and see what's what."

"You shouldn't have any trouble in this," La Rouch said as he patted the top of the car.

"I shouldn't be too late sir."

"How long is too late?"

"Not past midnight."

"Right," La Rouch said cautiously. "What I wanted to tell you was the Major wants you to go with him tomorrow so be ready by 0:700 hours. He'll be here to pick you up."

"Right sir," Wilkins said as he glanced at his watch. It was nearly five and he had promised to pick up Mai by five thirty.

"So who's this contact?"

"Can't say right now sir, but you know the major, all his little secrets and things?"

La Rouch drew in a breath like it was a kind of recognition of the fact and turned to leave.

Wilkins watched for a second then poured on the gas. The Lada shoved some gravel from under its back tire. It was the only example of mechanical might the Soviets could put into their vehicles for the masses.

The Sergeant had no compunction to go directly to Mai's house. Anyone in civilian clothes and driving a Lada couldn't be a threat to anyone in particular.

CHAPTER 10

Dmitri was fuming. How could so many things go wrong with such simplicity? Put the combine on a truck drive it to the demonstration area and wait for the signal to start harvesting.

Who could have guessed that the first truck would go off the road trying to avoid a head on with a water buffalo, and the second one having three flat tires after running over the boxes of nails being carried by the water buffalo. If it wasn't for the fact the third combine was five hours late, it too would have been inoperable. But that wasn't the worst of it.

The farm that had been picked for the demonstration wasn't very far from the city. It was picked for convenience sake of the North's officials who would be attending. Unfortunately, the oats that had grown and were left to be harvested had been beaten down by the monsoon rains and laid perpendicular with the ground. It wasn't about cutting it off near the root but scooping it up from the mud. Moreover, just across the border there were several oat fields that were ready for harvesting and growing in considerably dryer climates.

There was a knock at the office door and Dmitri looked up just as Proust entered with a letter in his hand.

"A communique from the Commissar of Agriculture sir," Proust said as he walked directly to the desk and laid it before the frustrated official.

Dmitri reached over and picked up the corner and viewed the contents with contempt.

"Oh God, they at least could spell my name right!" Dmitri said was he laid the letter down.

"But sir, they are praising you on your demonstration." Proust said as he leaned over his boss's beefy shoulder.

"We haven't had the demonstration yet. We'll be lucky if we get the damn machines to the fields. It would be easier to bring the fields to the machines!"

"Sir they don't know that back home and we can always claim a clerk's error if anyone finds out."

"Are you volunteering to be that clerk if it happens?"

Proust straightened at the thoughts of being held accountable. He joined the government for the very reason no one is ever held accountable for blunders.

"Perhaps we can create a diversion of sorts."

"Like?"

"Well we could announce some kind of diplomatic controversy, or some kind of extra marital entanglement. Perhaps one of the North's representatives in Moscow can be having sex with Gorbachev's daughter."

"You can arrange that?"

"A word in the right ear can do wonders Commissar." Proust boasted confidently.

"I think we should try to rescue this mess first," Dmitri said as he shoved the letter across his desk to an unoccupied corner left for discarded correspondence.

"Do we know if comrade Schenko is going to be here?"

"His office claims he arrived yesterday and should be at the Victory Hotel."

"Our man Ellermann, is he watching?"

"Yes sir, he has instructions to keep an eye on him."

"Good, inform Ellermann to stay close but far enough he can't be seen."

"Yes sir, right away," Proust said and disappeared from the room as quickly as he had arrived.

"I'll call over and let Schenko know were to be tomorrow!" Dmitri called out. He wasn't sure if Proust had heard him, but it really didn't matter much. Sometimes the lack of hearing things can be a blessing in disguise.

Dmitri picked up the receiver and heard the familiar sound of static electricity that seemed to fade in and out like waves on a beach. It was the first time in months the phone lines hummed the instant you picked up the receiver. The Americans had kept nearly all the wire on the ground, when it should be on the polls.

CHAPTER 11

Wilkins made good time getting to Mai's house, it was easy to find on the river road that paralleled Rout 6 about a mile away. There weren't any close neighbors and the vegetation that completely surrounded the small lot made it difficult for anyone to observe her comings and goings. The landmark was the lattice roof of the Jin Sing field across the street.

He pulled into the narrow driveway and parked the Lada in the single space in the side yard. Getting out, but keeping the engine running, Wilkins looked over the small homestead.

It was a pleasant place; the house was typical of small ranch houses in Hamilton except there was no garage attached. A line of red Radians filled the narrow space along the base of the house with the only interruption at the front door. There wasn't any grass, but long leafy pods sprang up everywhere giving the place a zero scape look.

Wilkins went to the door and knocked firmly, unlike Horst's knock that sounded more like a hiccup. Mai opened the door without hesitation; she was expecting him and had been dressed for more than an hour.

"Bless me Father," Wilkins said as he surveyed his date. "You look lovely Mai."

She smiled at the tallish Canadian dressed like he was on vacation at the beach.

"You want come in?"

"I think if I did, I'd never leave," Wilkins replied in a boyish tone.

She stepped back and retrieved a black shawl from the back of a chair. Wilkins followed and helped her put it on. It was then he took in her form, dressed in a light blue ankle length dress with the Guru collar she filled the garment neatly, nothing forcing the seams. Her hair was coiled on top of her head and the slippers she wore had beaded dragons on the tops. The shawl added a sense of mystique to her appearance.

He stood like a granite stone gazing at her. He couldn't see the soldier he once worked with, instead she was a flower of a woman, and should be someplace else.

"Where we have diner?" Mai's words broke her spell on him.

"I don't know," Wilkins replied. He had been so caught up in having a date he forgot to get a reservation at any of the restaurants.

Mai smiled, her head turned slightly like she didn't understand his reply. Her eyes met his and she could see the confused look. In an instant she recalled a date she had while in college. The boy who picked her up was a blind date type and he too looked dazed. She was beginning to think all Canadian men had the same affliction.

"You come," she said as she stepped toward the door. "My uncle have place up river from here."

Wilkins was like a lost puppy; he simple obeyed orders and hoped for the best.

*   *   *

La Rouch decided to take a ride to the airport to see Lieutenant Ho Buc. The thought of Buc's wife living in the United States was grinding slowly at his conscience and it had worn a good size hole in it. The information Horst had given him was still fresh in his mind even though it was a few months old now.

The night had begun its conclusion of the day as the blue pickup with the UN letters painted on the door rolled past the guard house at the gate and continued to the entry of the terminal building. The door to the terminal was propped open by a sick from a nearby tree and the mist that began to fall was chased away from the opening by the draft that flowed through the structure.

The Captain parked and turned off the engine. He was having second thoughts. Was this going to be an act of courage or an exercise in stupidity? He had no idea how Buc would react but to keep leading him on was a cruel gesture and would back fire on him if he ever wanted Buc to provide him with any new intelligence.

Taking a deep breath La Rouch slid from the front seat and entered the terminal. He could see Buc with several of his guards talking and laughing across the room by the former café that had gone out of business the day the French left. It was said the espresso machine boarded the same plane as the owner.

La Rouch went for the small desk Buc usually occupied and stood firmly before it as if he was on parade.

"Ah Captain," Buc said as he sauntered up like a gun slinger to a bar. "I have not seen you in long time?"

"Yes Lieutenant, I've been a bit busy lately."

"Yes, American keep you filling out reports?"

"Yes, there is that."

Buc went around and sat down behind his desk. He then opened the lower drawer and pulled out a rather large stack of letters wrapped with string to keep them together as one.

"I have mail if you can take."

"I'm afraid I can't do that anymore."

"You get trouble from boss?" he asked quickly as if he was already under suspicion from the higher-ups.

"Yes and no," La Rouch replied. He then took a more relaxed stance and leaned against the counter as if he was buying a ticket.

"I no understand."

"You see Lieutenant; your letters were picked up by the Americans down in Saigon."

"Americans! You dow me!" Buc yelled and his friends began to take notice. At that point Buc broke into a screaming taunt of the Canadian in his own language which La Rouch didn't understand.

The Captain looked around to see Buc's men begin to approach and thought a tactical withdraw would be prudent at this juncture.

Turning he started walking toward the door with Buc on his heals yelling obscenities and the guards laughing at whatever Buc was saying.

Outside La Rouch climbed into the truck and slammed the door. Buc was standing beside the truck yelling through the open window. But as the Captain began to roll the window up Buc suddenly regained his composure and put his hand over the edge of the glass to keep the window from closing.

"I'm sorry Lieutenant; I didn't know the Americans would get your letters. They were in our diplomatic pouch you see."

Buc smiled, he leaned closer so his friends that had gathered around the door of the terminal couldn't hear him.

"MY wife!"

"She's fine and so is your son. The Americans sent her to live with the rest of your family in America."

Buc's face was drained by what he heard and he almost looked whiter than La Rouch.

"I won't see again," Buc said softly. He was feeling gratitude and anger and resentment all at the same time. His heart felt like it was going to pound a hole in his chest.

La Rouch tried to think of something consolatory to say but nothing came to him. He was beginning to feel the same pain as Buc but in a much lesser way. He truly couldn't appreciate the loss of a relative even though it was just across the ocean.

Buc's family would take care of his wife and son and they were free from the war that kept banging on her doorstep every day.

The invasion that still kept juggernauting its way toward the South's capital could only end if the Americans could stop it, and then what. Another attack again next year and the year after until all was wiped clean?

Buc knew like all of those in the north that the only way to stop hostilities was to stop hostilities and sign a peace agreement, but communist leaders were making too much money to worry about the consolidation of the country. That's was Uncle Hoa's dream, not theirs.

La Rouch revved the motor and as he did Buc stepped away. The truck pulled back and reversed direction heading for Group 6 leaving the Lieutenant struggling with a host of emotions.

CHAPTER 12

If it hadn't been for the four cars parked beside the French style house, Wilkins could never have guessed it was a functioning restaurant. And if Mai hadn't been there to show where the driveway was off the river road he would have missed it completely.

The two left the Lada near the driveway and walked toward the building. Wilkins was surprised to see that the overall design was the same as their Group 6 compound, but slightly smaller. The windows on the main floor were shuttered and no light entered the approach to the front door. Vines of some description had climbed the outer walls and the leafy green covered the more serious damage from previous years of decay.

Mai knocked at the door when they were present and a small woman answered, her graying hair gave the grandma effect perfectly. The old woman smiled and allowed the two to enter and she took them to a small table in a dining room off the main entry. There was a fire going in the hearth and it warmed the room nicely. Low watt bulbs in the chandelier gave off just enough ambience to find everything on the table.

Wilkins helped Mai with her chair and then seated himself close to her. From out of nowhere a waiter arrived with a bottle of wine and poured it into the small glasses on the table. The dishes were still absent, but would come with the meal later. It was customary to have a short drink before dining.

"This is some place," Wilkins exclaimed in a whisper.

"My uncle own it for long time. Even when French were here."

"Not many people come out this way eh?"

"Some come often; others not."

Wilkins glanced out the wall length window to his left and could see the lights blazing in the night sky from the military base down river. It gave him a reference as to where he was. It seemed the base was half way between Mai's house and the eatery.

It was then that three large men entered the room being led by the old woman. She walked them to their table at the far end of the room. As they passed Wilkins recognized one of the men. It was Colonel Chin from the airport. The other two men were white and very rotund.

Once they were seated Wilkins tried to overhear their conversation but it was carried on in low monotones of measurement.

"Do you know men?" Mai asked curiously because Wilkins attention was being brought to bear on the small group.

"I know one of them, it's Colonel Chin. He's in charge of airport security."

"I think he Chinese. His father dead and mother lives in Shanghai."

"You know him too eh?"

"Yes, man ask me to watch him long time ago. I did research and learned much about him."

"What man?"

"Someone from long time ago, he not here anymore."

Mai was playing coy simply because she didn't want Wilkins to know she was still working for Horst as an agent. The East German didn't really put too much emphasis on her to produce information because he had fallen for her himself. But over time the relationship was purely amicable, yet he still protected his relationship with her.

An older waiter percolated up to the table and Mai, without hesitation ordered the food for the two of them. Wilkins wasn't sure what he was getting but trusted the source implicitly.

"I wonder what he's doing here?" Wilkins asked causally as if trying to unravel a mystery that didn't really exist, at least for the moment.

"Business with Russians. Money move fast under table." Mai said with a grin. She was all too familiar with the dealings of foreigners and the way favors were returned.

"You know they're Russians?"

"Only by sight. They dress same way."

Mai raised her glass of wine and looked as if she was going to propose a toast. Wilkins did the same and instead of babbling something of unimportance they simply took a sip. But the look in each other's eyes was more than a simple acknowledgement; it had mutual fascination in it.

Over the course of the meal that lasted forty five minutes, they talked about a lot of familiar things. She told him of her childhood which was more advantageous for her than the others in her school. She didn't come from peasant stock and was always favored by her teachers, and rightly so. Mai was a very astute young girl who knew street smarts as well as the others. She was teased from time to time by those less fortunate for being a fence sitter. But years earlier her father taught here the value of diplomacy which came in handy more times than could be counted.

Wilkins on the other hand went on and on about his small town in Ontario. Not far from Brantford he talked about the winters and Mai chimed in with her experiences in Alberta. It was an attempt at agreement to the hostile cold, but it came out more like up-man-ship. "The air was so cold if you said something outside you had to bring it inside to thaw out so you could hear what was said,' type of thing.

It was then Wilkins noticed her smile. The scar on her chin was barely visible in the dimmed light, but her lips formed the most perfect curve. Her dark eyes seemed to flow right through him when he looked at her. Trying to tell a lie to her face would be ever so impossible and Wilkins prayed that day would never come.

They finished their meal and Wilkins left an overly abundant tip, more for the uninterrupted time than the food and service.

They left the building and he drove her home. When they arrived he walked her to the door.

Wilkins had good manners for a GI, and even the French would have remarked about his politeness and gentlemanly manner. Because of his size, he also possessed a form of clumsiness when around women, especially those much smaller than he.

They stood looking at one another after Mai opened the door and the subdued light of her home blessed the sides of the faces.

Wilkins wanted to try a kiss but couldn't seem to get over the pounding in his chest. Mai also felt something, she had rarely felt before.

It was then Wilkins mustered enough courage to take her right hand and bring it to his lips. A gentle caress and the moment was over. It felt a lot like the ending of his high school final exam. And like that moment, he felt a sudden exhilaration, but he kept his composure.

"I had good time Sergeant."

"I did to eh."

Wilkins took a few steps back and then paused asking, "When are you off next?"

"I think Saturday."

"You haven't seen your father in a while have you?"

"No, why you ask."

"Oh nothing, just wondered that's all."

Wilkins smiled and tossed her a salute. It wasn't traditional, just a friendly gesture.

CHAPTER 13

It was to be a glorious day, if only one thing went right, Dmitri thought as he finished shaving. His apartment was only blocks from the Hungarian Embassy and he usually walked to work. Even during monsoon an English made umbrella was adequate protection. The only problem was he kept leaving it at the wrong place. It was either in his cloakroom at the office when he was at home, or at home when he was at the office. It was once suggested that he buy a dozen of them, but that was completely out of the question on a Commissars pay. And it didn't look good to have such lavish accessories lying around for the boss to see.

The gray light of morning met him as he stepped out into the street. He walked briskly to his office and arrived before Proust, his assistant. That was one of the attributes of Dmitri; he was always ahead of his assistants, if for no other reason than to point a bent figure at their tardiness.

But when he arrived at his workplace the room was already occupied by Commissar Schenko, of the Industrial Workers Directorate. Schenko was seated on the sofa with the large picture of Gorbachev prominently nailed to the wall behind him. It was necessary to hang large pictures like that because of the weak plaster coatings offered little support.

"Ahh Commissar, good morning to you!" Dmitri said as he entered his office. He walked briskly over to shake the hand of the attending observer who was charged with gaging Dmitri's performance of his duties.

Schenko merely waved off the gesture, it was to common place for suck ups which he had grown tired of. His status in the Politburo made him lazy and bored. He loved making underlings sweat, it was the only thing to look forward to when rounding agencies.

"Is our car ready?" Schenko said.

Dmitri, stunned by the lack of warmth from his superior held up his finger in a eureka fashion moment and shot for the phone to call the motor pool.

A few seconds later Dmitri announced the car was waiting and the driver eager to get started before the daily round of harassment by American fighters showed up.

The two bureaucrat's headed for the lower level garage below the embassy which doubled as the air raid shelter. As Dmitri led the way to the black Mercedes he spotted Major Ellermann standing by the exit door. A black Lada was idling and this was apparent by the blue smoke coming from the tail pipe.

*   *   *

Major Tennyson had already made arrangements to meet Sergeant Wilkins at the compound the day before and as predicted the Sergeant was standing on the porch of the chateau at the appointed hour.

Wilkins, steal feeling somewhat giddy from the night before and his date with Mai, bounced into the vehicle before it had made a complete stop. The Major was nearly sat on by the tall NCO and quickly leaned to one side. Once seated; the two made themselves more comfortable.

Tennyson looked at the man beside him and made the comment, "What is that on your lip Wilks?" The Major called the sergeant that as a form of nickname, it was intended to be respectful.

The Sergeant reached up and wiped his lip thinking he must have missed a piece of breakfast.

"Did I get it sir?"

"No its still there," Tennyson said. "It looks like a smile of some sort."

"Sorry sir."

"Are you starting to like your job Wilk's?"

"No sir, I just had a night of relaxation."

"I see. La Rouch didn't include that in his report of what I sent you out on. He was quite put back that you didn't include him in your secret mission."

"I'm sorry sir, I didn't know I muffed up on this one."

"Please take a moment before you go out to think up a really good lie to tell him in future."

"Yes sir I will."

"Good."

The two leaned back and Wilkins starred out the window for a time, the smile was growing into a devilish grin and he didn't want the Major to observe his lack of restraint.

It wasn't clear as to why Tennyson was called out to the demonstration point where he would meet up with Assistant Director Roth. The Canadians never had to worry about other countries making such efforts to break into the business of providing combines to the North. Especially when the inadequate machines came from the Soviets.

CHAPTER 14

Some Greek once said, 'I can see a lot farther when I'm standing on the shoulders of Giants,' and to that end, those gathering at the small farm to watch the demonstration of Soviet technology were in for a surprise.

Typically the inviting party will erect a small platform for the dignitaries to observe from, but that wasn't the case. Instead a hay wagon was dragged onto the edge of the field by the road, and those arriving lined both sides of the thoroughfare with cars and jeeps making a bottleneck for traffic. The selected observers where motioned by police to head for the wagon if they wanted to see anything.

From the viewing position the field, which was about 20 acres in size and similar to a mall parking lot, had very little change in the terrain. It was flat enough to make into a golf course if anyone had the money. The only problem was the wheat that was supposed to be standing upright was in a terrible declining position. The ground itself wasn't designed for wheat growing as it was previously a rice paddy and had all the characteristics of a muddy bog.

Dmitri was holding court on his farm implement dais with Schenko standing like a granite column beside the Hungarian. He was surrounded by several of the North's agricultural commissars.

Roth and Lock from the Canadian embassy were there along with Tennyson and Wilkins who stood in the back and played the role of innocent bystanders. But there were two other men there who were unknown to the security force of the Major and NCO. They said very little and watched intently.

When all were present Dmitri signaled Proust to call on the radio to the barn for the combines to make their appearance. The sky threatened rain but looked to be holding off for a more opportune time.

There was a rumbling of distant thunder but it was only the combines starting their engines. The barn the equipment was stored in made the perfect echo chamber and those trying to flee the noise had to drive out of the menace to the ears. The clouds of diesel smoke didn't help much either.

The observers watched the three mechanical giants headed down the short driveway and turn onto the paved road. The Hungarian technical chief that was in charge of the operational effectiveness of the equipment walked ahead of the convoy as if he were the band master. Waving his arm to indicate the direction of the turn he shuffled along with the leading machine nearly running him over when he slowed and the machine didn't.

With engines screaming and the clatter of metal banging away at itself the procession made for the field. But what couldn't go unnoticed even if you were deaf was the fact the tires made a terrible roaring sound on the pavement, even at slow speeds. It was obvious to most that there was something wrong with the tires. Perhaps they thought; the tires were under inflated.

Finally the machines reached the field and drove in one behind the other to take up an echelon formation which would be the typical arrangement when in full harvest. It was here the tech left the vehicles and climbed up onto the hay wagon to join the dignitaries.

Dmitri was too curious and asked the obvious question. "Why are they so loud?"

"The tires are on backwards," The tech called over the sound of the engines at full throttle.

Everyone watch as the three yellow beasts make a futile attempt to harvest the flattened wheat. Mud flew up from under the equipment like sows rampaging for the trough.

After a run down one side of the field the three implement's made a turn to head back but for some reason the machines began to swerve wildly in all directions. It wasn't because the drivers had lost control it was part of the demonstration to show off the maneuverability even in muddy conditions.

"The tires are on backwards?" Dmitri called out with a grin trying not to show his surprise as his boss was standing beside him.

"The tread on the tires are from a new design. Before the tread was shaped like a 'V', now it's like a reversed 'T'"

"Then change them around."

"We can't the tires are on the rims the wrong way and we don't have the equipment to flip them." The tech replied in a lower tone. "Besides it wouldn't make any difference anyway."

The origination of the problem began a year earlier when the tire manufacture in Romania came up with a revolutionary design. But instead of filing the proper paperwork and the consuming time of regulation approval, the manufacture simply forged the signatures to the proper forms and sent the tires onto the combine company. The tires were installed as part of the assembly and never recalled.

As the group watched with interest the three machines began doing some kind of dodge ball tactics, only without a ball. They swerved and ran toward each other then turned sharply at the last minute and rolled around to do it again. All this rousting began to take its toll on the field. Huge tracks from the oversized tires crisscrossed each other and it was starting to look more like a construction site.

Roth looked over at Lock and whispered, "Have we got anything to worry about?"

"Are you kidding," Lock replied with a grin.

Lock who was the Agricultural officer for the Canadians had seen some malevolent demonstrations but this one would take the cake.

"It would seem someone forgot to bring the soccer ball sir," Wilkins said sarcastically.

The Major merely looked over and made his reply with a wink.

It was then that a flight of two American F-4 Phantoms whipped past low enough to see the pilot's faces. The aircraft streaked over the three machines like hawks looking for lunch.

A panic broke out as the dignitaries ran for their respective transportation. Dmitri turned to help Schenko down from the cart but the commissar was already climbing into the Mercedes.

Turning his eyes skyward, the Hungarian was beginning to realize he should have spent more time with the Catholics.

The Canadians, instead of climbing into their vehicles were ordered by Tennyson to take cover away from the road behind an earth berm that formed the ditch. The road was jammed with traffic which included the usual civilian commuters. No one was going anywhere.

The jets made a complete turn taking several miles to execute the maneuver and went into attack mode. Instead of bullets from the mini-guns, the two jets fired half a dozen rockets which fanned out and encircled the combines like Indians at the Little Big Horn. When they impacted, exploding mud was hurled like rain down onto the machines that had now come to a halt. The drivers jumped from their rigs and ran for cover between the detonating rockets.

As quickly as they came the jets left with only vapor trails to mark their retreat.

Dmitri paused by the door of his car and looked out into the field. The combines were still running as black smoke belched from the exhaust. He could make out the drivers going back to make another stab at impressing the dignitaries, but most had already mingled with the slow moving civilians heading home.

Dmitri climbed into the back seat of the car beside Schenko who looked like he had really swallowed something nasty, and tried to garner some hope with a halfhearted smile.

In an instant the face of one of the North's generals, decorations dangling like trinkets in a bazaar appeared in the door window.

Dmitri cranked down the glass.

"Yes General?" Dmitri said curiously.

"We want buy, now much?"

Dmitri felt like there was a God and he wasn't still back in Moscow or wherever Communist God's go.

"How many machines do you want General?" Dmitri asked with glee.

"Don't want machines want tires. I send you order for three thousand tomorrow."

The officer hurried back to his waiting car that went in the opposite direction.

Dmitri looked over at Schenko who was smiling with tight squinting eyes.

"It would seem you have made a sale comrade," Schenko said. "Proust! To my hotel and we all have lunch together. I must get to know you better Dmitri."

As the black Mercedes pulled itself from the softened shoulder the two strangers could see the disillusioned face of a Hungarian commissar hoping the war would be over soon.

*　　*　　*

Horst and Werner stood firm on their little perch beside the road watching the Mercedes disappear into the flood of travelers. To their left the Canadians were beginning to stand erect and view the debacle of the combines still in the field.

The Hungarian tech was running toward the machines in an attempt to end the collective mayhem.

The day before Werner had contacted Horst to rent a car for the trip out to the farm. He was to wear a shirt and tie, something a clicker isn't comfortable doing. Werner made no specific demands except to keep it as secret as possible. Horst had no idea as to why he was being dragged along so he just convinced himself into believing he was just a lackey.

The East German's car was farther down the road, not because they were late but because they didn't want to look like they were a part of the observation group.

The Canadians were now moving toward their transportation and Werner made a quick paced lunge toward Lock and Roth. He knew just which people he wanted to talk to. Horst remained where he was as the Major and Sergeant paused to intervene if necessary.

"Mister Roth mister Lock, I'm Werner Munnt," the East German announced civilly in a broken English accent.

"Yes mister Munnt," Roth said holding out his hand.

The gesture was received in a firm manner as Werner also connected with Lock.

"It voud appear the Soviets have a vays to go yes?"

"We're not too concerned about this," Lock answered.

"Ya, it would seem dat the Soviet machines are useless in monsoon."

"Well honestly, mister Pskov would have had a better show if he planned it for the harvest season. About three months ago this might have proven to be trouble for us." Roth said.

"I voud also say the cost for such machines would be too much?"

"Perhaps, but I think the North isn't taking that into consideration at this time."

"And vy?"

"Well the North has just raised its agricultural budget by twenty percent for this year." Lock said in an attempt to be knowledgeable on such topics . . .

"By the way, who did you say you were with?" Roth asked curiously

"Oh Ya, I'm sorry I'm with East German Agriculture."

"Then I think we should be going," Roth said as he slapped Lock on the shoulder. "Before you give away any more secrets," he added laughingly.

It wasn't much of a secret, but it did give Werner food for thought.

No other communication was exchanged between the five men except when the Major eyed Werner a bit questioningly as he passed.

Once inside his car, the Major ordered the driver to make for Group 5.

"We're going to see your buddy Sergeant," Tennyson said as he made himself comfortable.

"What occasion do we have for that sir?"

"I have to inform Bishop he's under house arrest until further notice."

"For his work on the guard at the gate I take it?"

"Yes Sergeant, and other things that need to be sorted out."

"Yes sir."

"By the way, what did you think of that German fellow back there?"

"I would say he's just another bureaucrat, why?"

"Well Captain La Rouch was contacted by a German last week and the description didn't fit this mister Munnt. But it might have fit the other man with him."

Wilkins glanced out his window as if he was going to get a look at Horst, but they were too far away for anything exact. And added to that was the clustering of motor cycles and people on bicycles amassing their car as everyone tried to get on.

"I didn't pay that much attention to the other man sir."

"That's alright," Tennyson said. "He probably isn't a very big fish anyway."

CHAPTER 15

From the demonstration area near Cam Son Lake to route 10 that went toward the three temples bridge the driver made a small error in direction and cost the ride another hour. This wasn't that big of a deal to Tennyson and Wilkins, but it did indicate how easy it was to get turned around even in flat coastal terrain. The key was to remember the various pagodas on the way. If you see one you've seen before, you're in trouble.

Tennyson got to know more about Wilks, or Sergeant Wilkins. It was a sort of nickname he had attached to the Sergeant as a force of habit. The Major tended to give a badge of distinction to the men he liked. He also reiterated the Sergeants promotion and pointed out he needed a good NCO chief to make the machine move better. This meant that Wilkins could stitch the crown between the 'V' of his stripes. His next promotion would be to Warrant Officer First if it was deemed necessary.

Just before the intersection of route 18 and route 10 they had to stop for a passing train headed west from Gieng Day which was about six miles from the major city of Halong.

Gieng Day had been deepened to accept ocean going ships but the channel wasn't wide enough to accommodate many of the large vessels. In fact, only one ship at a time could be docked and unloaded which meant the cargo was of top priority to the North. And because the jungle hugged the water's edge on two sides, the ship was nearly invisible to air observation. Additionally the small harbor was on one of the estuaries and the surrounding land was high enough to not be a problem with flooding. The North had run a rail line down to the harbor to accelerate shipments to Hanoi. Most of the rail line had been built under double canopy jungle which suggested the trains weren't seen except when they crossed an open road. The problem for the track layers was trying to keep it under the trees.

From the town it did seem funny to look over the tree tops and spot the mast of the cargo cranes on the ship looming up like so many flag poles.

It wasn't a secret port and it was indicated on many charts, but due to its location and distance from Hai Phong it usually went unnoticed by Navy pilots hungry for a clean kill.

As the train slowly rolled passed struggling under the load the two scanned the various rail cars for any indication of the type of cargo. There were many box cars and a few petroleum cars, but a steady line of flat cars with long narrow wooden containers with red stars painted one them brought up the rear.

Unlike Canadian trains there was no caboose, just a man sitting on one of the boxes with a yellow flag in his hand. But because it was a single mainline there was no chance of a rear end collision.

"What do you think Wilks?" Tennyson asked casually as he leaned back in his seat.

"I haven't a got a clue sir, without looking inside. But an educated guess would be SAM missiles for the defensive ring around Hanoi."

"Unassembled of course?"

"Yes sir."

"I'm wondering if Captain Scott has seen the ship bringing the stuff in?"

"It would be under his jurisdiction sir, Group 5 is responsible for all shipping around Hai Phong."

"I think he would know that Wilks, but what I'm concerned about is the delay in getting the new basecamp up and running. Not only is Gieng Day over sixty miles away by water, but he would have to make a special trip to check things out. And no chance of buying any fuel on the way."

"Why doesn't he just drive over sir?"

"Because Group 5 is a Marine unit and has to arrive by sea in order to be authorized to do a search. Besides, he's so far off anyone watching the coast who saw him would know exactly where he's going and they could hide the stuff before he got there."

"I see, doesn't seem fair."

"But when is it fair Wilks?"

Wilkins watched the last of the train roll by and leaned back in his seat beside the Major. The car rolled over the bumpy tracks and for once was leading the pack of motorbikes and trucks, not to mention the throngs of travelers on bicycles.

At the village of Bieu Nghi the road intersected with the way south to Three Temples. Traffic became considerably lighter because most were going to Halong.

It was only eleven miles to Quang Yen and the river crossing. From there it would be a mile or so to Group 5.

*   *   *

"I'm going to assign you a special project Horst," Werner said as the two were riding back to the rental car office.

"I'm just a clicker heir Munnt, not a field man."

"This is under your job description heir Volkmann," Werner ordered, he could sense Horst reluctance to anything out of the ordinary. Most of the lower ranks didn't do well when sequestered for a special assignment. But that was the usual case and it was expected.

"I may have to get permission from head office sir."

"Head office is not to know of this. Besides I told you who I am. Why are you insubordinate. You are German, you follow orders yes?"

"Sir I work for a magazine in Berlin. I have a boss too you know?"

"You work for the CIA as do I and Otto. The magazine is only a cover."

"Yes sir! Heir Munnt."

"Then you will do as ordered yes?"

"Yes sir," Horst replied in disgust. He knew it wasn't good to argue with those who are in another cell, or loop.

"I'm going to Hong Kong on tomorrow, Otto is not to know of this. I should be back by the following Wednesday. While I'm gone I want you to follow and take pictures of Commissar Schenko. He over see's transfer payments to Moscow. I have been told he is here to see the North's Chief Directorate and make new arrangements for war payments."

"He's pretty important yes?"

"Yes."

"Then he will have a shadow man yes?"

"Most possible yes."

"I think I know who the shadow man is. Ellermann. He used to be with the Stassi in Berlin."

"Then make sure he doesn't see you."

"I'll handle it sir."

"Good, then I'm free to do my job."

"Will you need a ride to the airport sir?"

"No, I'll take a taxi."

"It might be less observable if you arrive in unmarked car sir. I can drop you in the parking lot. I'll hold over the rental until tomorrow."

Werner paused before answering. He knew Horst was right because he it was part of his training at Langley to use the least obvious means of transportation when necessary.

"Very well. My flight leaves at noon."

Horst nodded his reply and a small grin began to form on his lips. It wouldn't be noticed by his boss he thought. Werner wouldn't have made a good field man, in his opinion.

CHAPTER 16

It didn't take all that long to arrive on the road to Group 5. The compound lay and the end of a muddy path widened for vehicle traffic and which tended to flood during monsoon when the rivers expand their domain. In fact, Group 5 was on a small rise and was more like an island than a spit of land running through a swamp. The only good thing was the camp was high enough to see over the long grass which made it nearly impossible to sneak up on, even at night. Visibility was miles in distance.

For the driver there were several turns to the wheel to avoid pot holes the size of tennis courts, but after a while they arrived and drove through the open gate that was unattended. Scott was confident about his surroundings and because all that was there at Group 5 was a few vehicles and boat, it wasn't much of a target for anyone.

The driver parked the Chrysler sedan near the door of the concrete building being used as Scott's headquarters and billets. Tennyson patted him on the shoulder as a signal he needn't get out.

"Right Wilks, lets pay our respects." Tennyson said as he slid from his rear seat out onto the muddy ground. It was mostly sand and dry enough so it wouldn't stick to their leather shoes.

The two entered the office and Scott snapped to attention from behind his desk.

"Good to see you sir," Scott said not making a salute. He didn't have his hat on so it wasn't required.

"At ease Captain, Tennyson said as he shifted over and took a metal folding chair and dragged it to the left of the desk. He them carefully lowered himself into it.

"Nice to see you Sergeant Wilkins."

"Yes sir."

"Is Bishop handy Captain?"

"He's in the motor pool sir working on our three quarter ton. He thinks it's a carburetor problem."

"He knew we were coming didn't he?"

"Oh yes sir," Scott said as he seated himself.

"I'll go and get him sir," Wilkins said as he nearly ran to exit the room. He was anxious to see his friend again. It had been nearly three weeks.

As Wilkins made for the shed used as a garage the two officers made conversation that was cordial in nature.

"So are you getting it together down here?"

"Yes sir, in most respects we're fully operational. The Vergil has been shaken out and everything from the old compound is here and nearly set up, thanks to the Corporal's handy work."

"Good, how's he been doing?"

"He's keeping it together as best he can sir."

"How do you mean?"

"Well," Scott began as he folded his hands in front of him on the desk. "Early on the men complained about him a bit, and so we got him to build an NCO room for himself."

"Well he is an NCO and he should be bunking away from the men."

"Yes sir, but that wasn't really the intended point of the maneuver if you see my point?"

"Not very clearly Captain."

"Well sir, Bishop occasionally cries in his sleep."

Tennyson paused, he knew the signs of battle fatigue and uncontrolled crying spells was one of the first signs of too much war.

"Anything else?"

"The only explanation he gave to Kirk was that it was his anniversary period."

"Anniversary of what?"

"If you recall sir, it was about this time last year when he was with the US forces at Khe Sanh during Lam Son 719. And you know they got hammered pretty good out there."

"Yes, I read the after action reports from Saigon. The South lost half of its best men."

"Yes sir, and its gradually getting worse by inches."

"How worse?"

"Well so far it's only been the crying and a few words that none of the men can understand. He sleeps under his blanket so they can't hear everything."

"How's his temperament?"

"He flies off the handle now and then for what seems like no good reason, but other from that, he's a good soldier. In fact he's better than good. If you had seen the look on the face of the North's Captain on the patrol ship the other day when Bishop threatened to shoot him. All I can say is, I'm glad he wasn't pointing it at me. I'd have died from a heart attack."

"Yes he has good reflexes that's for sure."

"Do you think he's becoming a problem sir?"

"Bishop is always a problem, I'm down here to advise him of the court's ruling from his last fiasco."

"Is it severe sir?"

"Hardly, he has to turn over a month's pay, but that will probably get lost in finance so he's off again. I suspect in about twenty years he might miss half a month's cash out."

"Damn good efficiency in the Army eh sir?"

"The usual thing."

"Can I offer you some coffee sir. Wilkins should be on his way back by now?"

*   *   *

Sergeant Wilkins had found Bishop bent over the engine compartment of the Group's smallest truck. The duce and a half was parked beside it ready to roll. It was the Corporal's duty to make sure the land transport was always ready. But the small truck was the most frustrating because of its age.

When Wilkins spotted his friend he had just rounded the corner of the building. Thinking it would be a good joke to surprise him he yelled out at the top of his voice, "BISHOP!"

In one split second the Corporal swung around and released the screw driver he had in his hand which flew across the twenty feet of open space and buried the tip in the side of the building.

"Judas Priest Bishop!" Wilkins called.

"Holy shit, sorry sarge I didn't know it was you," Bishop apologized as he stepped down from the truck.

"What the hell is the matter with you?"

"Just a little tense that's all," Bishop replied and added, "I'm really sorry sarge."

Shaken by the near miss, Wilkins who had ducked slightly straightened himself and went over to his friend.

"Do you know what time it is?" Wilkins asked.

Bishop glanced up at the faint glow of the sun through overcast clouds and said, "It's part way through the day. A day is part of a week. A week is part of a month, and a month is part of a year. And with nothing to look forward to, who the fuck cares?"

"The Major's here to see you," Wilkins replied as he stood before his friend.

"Ah shit, is that today?"

"You got it mister."

"Okay, hold him off while I get changed," Bishop replied as he step passed his friend and went towards the barracks and his room to put on a clean uniform.

Wilkins paused and watched as the Corporal walked away. He almost felt sorry for the Corporal and he knew what it was like to try to avoid contact with officers. Nothing good hardly ever came from the meeting. And his news about his date with Mai would also have to wait.

CHAPTER 17

It was quite in Captain Scott's office when Bishop knocked on the door. He had been standing there for a few seconds listening through the wooden barrier trying to get an idea of how the conversations were going, but nothing had given him a clue. The voices were muffled to the point there was no chance to identify an exact word.

The Corporal knocked and when response was given he marched in and stood at attention in front of the Captains desk. He noticed the Major sitting to his left and Wilkins leaning against a window sill to his right.

Both officers eyed him carefully. Bishops neat uniform was in proper discipline for parade dress. Everything that could be polished was and the overall impression was of a professional soldier who may have been a little too experienced.

"At ease Corporal," Tennyson said with a grin.

Bishop complied but said nothing. He knew it was always better to not say anything unless spoken directly to. It was a habit that kept him out of trouble, at least in the beginning of the conversation.

The Major took a paper from his pocket and began to read the list of charges against him for assaulting a member of the North Vietnamese Security Police. It read the date and the particulars. Then the sentence and fine.

"I assume you would have pleaded guilty if you were there." Tennyson said smiling.

"That depends sir, did they have any proof it was me. It was pretty dark that morning sir."

"How do you spell congratulations Corporal?"

"Sir?"

"Spell the word please."

"Ah, c o n g r a d e y o u l a s i o n s."

"That's what I thought, you're guilty."

"I told you, you didn't spell it right," Wilkins said with a grin.

"So what are you going to do, send me to Vietnam?" Bishop barked back.

"Settle down Corporal," Scott ordered as he tried to hide his laughter.

"Right," Tennyson said as he stood up. "Gentlemen would you give us some private time."

Scott and Wilkins complied and as they turned for the door Bishop moved with them.

"Not you Corporal," Tennyson ordered.

"I thought you wanted to talk to the Captain Sir . . ."

"No, it's you I want."

The Major seated himself on the edge of the desk a few feet from the Corporal. He crossed his arms and looked directly at the NCO.

"I guess I screwed up again." Bishop said apologetically.

"I have found that in poker, you can't win big without losing a hand or two."

"That's just it sir, I'm not really winning anything."

"I wouldn't say that. You've been pretty competent in you extra activities. The proof is your success in completing the mission. And Wilks thinks pretty highly of you."

"Wilkins is a good man sir. Needs a little more experience though."

"How do you mean?"

"Well sir, it's been my experience that if you ever threaten a man with a gun it's better to shoot him in the leg and send him home."

Bishop was referring to the incident at the Laos and North Vietnam border when he wanted to take the POW's all the way to the landing zone. Wilkins pulled his pistol and ordered Bishop to not go over, and because the Corporal respected his Sergeant, he didn't. But if he had been with the Americans it would have been a totally different outcome.

"Do you remember that day when I got you out of jail down by Group 2?"

"Yes sir."

"Do you remember how I told you to get the job done but don't make waves?"

"Yes sir, am I making waves?"

"I wouldn't say waves as yet, but you are getting noticed, especially by the Americans. Those men on the Forrestal knew who you were, and soon the North is going to know as well."

"Yea that got me thinking too sir."

"Right, so keep your head down more."

"Yes sir."

"Now I have something for you to do."

Bishop changed his foot position because it was beginning to hurt to stand at ease. It wasn't a position his body was used to.

"With the invasion going on down south," Tennyson began as he moved from the desk to his chair and reseated himself. "The North is getting more and more equipment into the battle from their neighbors. The Americans are keeping the railroads torn up, so the only way through is by sea. Now the Americans are thinking about mining the harbor but WE wouldn't stand for that."

"They just might go ahead and do it anyway sir, for the hell of it if nothing else."

"Right, I've thought of that, but the mining only concentrates the vessels in one area. They make great targets but the Americans can't hit them because the ships are under international protection from WARSAW PAC and NATO."

"If they're all bunched up that makes it easier for us to watch them."

"Right, but I need some hard evidence that the WARSAW PAC is sending more arms and munitions beyond the accords agreement."

"You mean under the Cease Fire Agreement they can still get guns and bullets?"

"One hundred tons a month"

"Shit, then what's the point?"

"Self-defense."

"Man the lawyer's were sure in on this one."

"Whatever the case," Tennyson said as he got up to leave. "There is plenty of opportunity for you to get noticed, so don't."

"Does this mean I'm going to be independent again?"

"When have I ever said that soldier?" Tennyson said with a wink.

"Can I use somebody out of Group 5?"

"If they agree, but I don't want to know about it right?"

"Yes sir."

The Major put on his beret and gave Bishop a salute. The Corporals hand started to return the courtesy, but stopped realizing he was being given a thumbs up so to speak.

CHAPTER 18

During the ride back to the embassy Wilkins queried the Major on his agenda for the next few days, particularly through the weekend. Tennyson was curious and asking a few not so direct questions he deduced the sergeant was up to something, and it was better if he didn't know all the facts.

Wilkins wanted to take Mai to see her father, it was a risk to say the least but the Sergeant figured it might be possible if the Lada was used instead of an official vehicle. Dressed like a Pol, he figured any sentries wouldn't argue.

Major Tennyson told of his business trip to Hong Kong leaving on Friday, which was the next day and gave Wilkins permission for a three day pass. Something that might come in handy if the Sergeant should be in the wrong place and ordered Wilkins to come up with a good cover story for the vacation time.

If that didn't work or the circumstances were of a unique nature Wilkins was to make it official and claim he was on a search mission for a possible secret missile site, but it was only a rumor and he was to make that clear to the North's interrogators should that even take place. The excuse for the Polish disguise was to make it easier to get the information clandestinely, which Wilkins could quote as Resolution 167-1962. Also, dressed as a Pol he could claim he deduced Mai into helping him and that would let her off the hook as it were.

Friday morning was overcast but the ceiling was over a thousand feet. Just as the NATO group boarded the Air Canada flight carrying them, the mail and dispatches to Hong Kong, a coincidence occurred that created a great deal of angst amongst those involved and those who would hear about it later.

The Major and mister Roth who had picked a widow seat had a clear view of the entire affair that lasted only fifteen minutes at best. The event began some three minutes earlier just as the Air Canada flight had lifted off the rutted runway and the wheels were retracted. The Air Canada pilots had overheard the radio conversations of the F-4 pilots and knowing the bombing was a considerable distance away took to the skies anyway.

An attack group of two F-4 Corsairs from the aircraft carrier USS Forrestal had just finished a run on a couple of poorly disguised fuel barges in the Red River and had destroyed the targets completely. The fault lay with the local commander who had used dark green summer camouflaged netting which stuck out like a sore thumb against the winter kill of the surrounding foliage.

When an attack group is formed it consists of a lead pilot and a wing man. In this instance, due to rotation, the lead pilot was as new as the wingman, but both pilots were very good at staying together like Chinese brothers. When they finished their attack the lead pilot missed a landmark and before he knew it they were nearly on top of the Air Canada flight. So they took evasive action which meant they slowed down and came up alongside the passenger plane as if to escort it out of the area.

There was some bravado on the lead pilot because he concluded that if they stayed close to the passenger plane then the antiaircraft batteries wouldn't try to shoot them down, and the trick worked. The three planes lazily headed for the coast like a couple of drunken sailors heading back to their ship.

Once at the coast the two fighters disengaged and headed straight back to the carrier.

By this time the diplomatic damaged had been insurmountable. The Canadian's claimed they had no connection to the fighters who obviously took advantage of the situation and used the passenger plane as cover. The North Vietnamese argued that this was a clear act by the US to protect its confederate which the North always claimed the Canadians did work of the Americans.

But all of this could have been avoided had the lead pilot rotated his map so NORTH was at the top of his chart.

In all wars zones any kind of incident like this would never be resolved and history would only prove that it can be written any way you like to support your opinion.

For Sergeant Wilkins the bombing was an opportunity he took full advantage of. By getting the damage reports and civilian casualty numbers from the area the fuel barrages were in, he was able to reach the hospital where Mai was at.

She had been transferred to another part of the facility because even the North could see that stress levels in the post operations section left everyone drained psychologically and that made things worse for the patients.

It took some time but Wilkins found the ward where Mai was working. It was on the back side of the hospital and the sound of planes passing over seemed to be less traumatic.

"You Wilkins why you here?" Mai asked as she turned away from a wounded soldier she was helping with a new dressing.

"I wanted to see you," Wilkins grinned; he was feeling that sense of boyishness that comes with a new venture of the heart.

"Where dumb shit?"

"Who?"

"Corporal?"

"Oh Bishop, he's still out on the coast, he'll be there a while eh."

"Why, he in trouble?"

"When isn't he in trouble?" Wilkins joked.

"You lock him up?"

"No nothing like that, just extra duty kind of thing. You know eh?"

"Yes, like me here."

"Yes that's right, now I want to tell you something," Wilkins said as he drew her with him behind a curtain. There was an empty bed so they had some privacy.

Wilkins lowered his voice to a whisper. "Now you said you had tomorrow off right?"

"Yes."

"Good, I've got a car and a pass so I'll drive you out to see your father if you like."

Mai's eyes lit up like fireworks. She hadn't been able to talk with her father in some time and the rumors of what was going on in the country from the invasion of the South were running rampant.

Even though the radio declared great victories by the North as they swept through the South's lines, there were starting to be large numbers of ambulances coming back loaded with wounded, and that was the worst cases. The rest had to walk home with the refugees.

"Yes I come with you, we leave early yes?"

"Right, I'll be there around seven."

Mai gave him a kiss on the cheek and disappeared around the curtain, certain to return to her duties but with more enthusiasm than before.

Wilkins stood for a moment, he was mesmerized by the gesture of affection, something he had forgotten existed for soldiers.

CHAPTER 19

O n overcast days it was black as coal, and on sunny days it was as brown as dirt, but it was consistently wet. The Bach Dang River was under threat of flooding and the waters had already moved into the bull rushes along the banks for many miles upstream above the Three Temples crossing. The Group 5 base was on a huge island known as Coc Lung Island that was south of the Three Temples and the town of Quang Yen. A gathering of other islands clustered around the biggest and was like a hen with her chicks around her.

Once the river had passed through the narrows of the Three Temples it broke out into the delta and had little effect on houses and business downstream. The major problem was the water flowing between the manmade dikes that fortified the river crossing making it look like the Colorado in spring.

Bishop and Greg, who was also the group cook, and a fine gourmet he was, planned a quick trip up to the market before their road to town was too deep to drive down. If the waters ever got excessive they would use the Vergil to make the run.

The three quarter ton truck sputtered to life as Bishop stepped on the starter. He dropped it into gear and pulled around to the main building where Greg was making out his food list. The engine noise got everyone's attention and they all reckoned there would be a good supper this evening.

"Corporal!" Captain Scott called from his office window and when Bishop spotted him he made the gesture for the NCO to see him before leaving.

Bishop put the truck in neutral and climbed out heading for Scott's office. As he stepped through the door he met Greg who was coming out.

"The boss wants something I'll be right back."

"Right Corp," Greg replied and seated himself on the passenger side.

"Where you headed?" Scott asked insistently when Bishop entered the office.

"Taking a run up to the market, Greg needs vegies for chow."

"Send him on I need you to go with us. We're making a quick check and peek."

"You don't need me for that sir."

"Normally your right, but the Major told me to guide you along as much as possible under the legal description of the Resolutions. And that means I might have something for you."

"I didn't think he meant the next day sir."

"The war waits for no man Corporal."

"I thought that was time sir."

"Not much difference I'd say Corporal."

"Okay sir, I'm with ya."

The two men left the office, Bishop told Greg to head on and the Vergil got underway with two sailors and two army personnel. It wasn't much of a deterring force, but it did have a purpose, but only Scott had a hunch as to what it might be.

*   *   *

Just about a half mile south of the base was where a channel broke away from the river forming Cam Ba Island, and just beyond that a much larger land fill called Qun Cong Island. The channel known as the ducks path meandered along the main part of the same island the base was on and had several pagodas stretched out like light houses heading toward the sea.

At one time they actually were employed as beacons for sea farers but after the war started the French realized their use as observation towers and shot off the tops of the pagodas so they couldn't be used to hold large lanterns or people. Even with twenty years of so called peace the pagodas were never rebuilt, but they were high enough to be seen from nearly any place in the delta.

Mike working as the helmsmen guided the Vergil through the channel nearly grounding the ship a couple of times. During monsoon the rivers current creates sand bars so quickly they can't be mapped because the next day they could be a hundred feet farther on. So Scott stood on the bow and directed Mike on which way to steer.

Progress was slow but in fact it was quicker because Qun Cong Island was miles across and to go around would have used up more fuel. The other benefit was the channel came out directly across from Din Voo a small town on the peninsula to Hai Phong harbor. This small town was a landmark Bishop committed to memory without hesitation.

Once free of the channel the Vergil set a course due west through the faster moving river current and in a half hour was rounding the spit of land known as finger point, marking the entrance to the bay. Stove fires from the village of Dinh

Voo filled the air with cedar smoke and it was one the most pleasant fragrances the jungle could produce.

The sound of two jet fighters roared passed far to the east and several miles out to sea. Bishop squinted into the slight mist and could just make out the vapor trails slicing through the low clouds and guessed they had just finished up something of importance and were headed back to the carrier for lunch.

As the small ship bore down on the entrance to Hai Phong and the maze of ship canals Bishop noticed two things to be very apparent. The first was there happened to be a dozen large ocean freighters anchored out in the wider part of the bay that emptied into the Gulf. The second was there were about five large freighters tied to moorings along the shore of the Cau Cam River leading to Hai Phong proper.

The main harbor for Hai Phong was nothing more than a stretch of docks and waterways with the city huddled on all sides of each water path. To get to the dockyards the ships had to navigate up the Cau Cam River and turn into a narrow channel. To get out the ships merely continued on until they reached the Tam Bac River and swung back into the main channel.

In a lot of ways Hai Phong was nearly an exact duplicate of Vung Tau with Saigon farther up river.

"I guess these guys are waiting to get unloaded in the harbor," Bishop said nodding to the line of ships moored to what looked like the bank

"In some ways they're already in the harbor and will be unloaded tonight when the tide goes out," Scott replied.

"What do you mean sir?"

It was then Bishop was provided with an historical account of the seaport town.

Scott began by telling of the French, when all of Vietnam was a colony prior to World War Two, and they came up with the notion of how to unload ships secretly so the town would not be bombed by the Japanese. History also tells that the French and the Japanese controlled the country together but that came after the sunken docks project.

Scott, a history major in college took pride in his deliverance of the historical doings and slowed the Vergil as to be able to point out items of interest related to his discussion.

The French decide to build huge rafts of logs cut and bound together and floated down stream to a site where pilings for ships were already sunk in the river bed. The log raft is tied in place and when the tide goes out the raft lies on the river bed that's now dry, but too soft to handle trucks. At the end of the raft a huge pot hole is dug so when the tide goes down the ship that's tied up settles into the dugout and remains afloat. Now trucks can drive out onto the raft and unload the cargo. When the tide comes in the trucks drive to the warehouse to unload. When tide goes out again they come back to the ship and reload it.

As time passed the raft became so waterlogged and was so heavy that it never moved as the tides changed.

The French designed it so Japanese planes couldn't bomb it because high tide occurs during the day. The Japanese pilots couldn't see the rafts because they were underwater. This meant the Japanese assumed that Hai Phong looked like a sleepy backwater town that could be taken without a shot fired.

"You got to handed it to the frogs, they sure know how to be sneaky," Bishop commented.

Scott went on to say that after the war the French still used the dock and let the local fishermen repair their fishing boats. Also at night, people would park their boats and have a party. They even orchestrated a fresh fish market that's lit up by hanging lanterns. Just enough light to see by but not enough to attract enemy aircraft. And today, nothing had changed.

Bishop was awed by the history lesson, he had always marveled at how the Vietnamese could take one thing and turn it to their favor. Like sandals from rubber tires.

The Vergil picked up speed and Bishop took a pair of binoculars and looked over the ships tied up along the bank. He could see the different flags flying from the sterns and most of the ships looked like they had already been through a couple of successful air raids by all the rust that was present. Perhaps he thought it was an intentional form of camouflage.

Bishop was scanning one of the tired freighters when he spotted a flag he didn't recognize.

"Hey sir, what countries that?"

Scott looked over in the general direction and said, "Venezuela."

Bishop noticed the ships name, the 'Guevara'. The last name of a communist rebel from Cuba sparked a remembrance.

"What the fuck!"

"What's the matter?" Scott queried.

"You know who Che Guevara was sir?"

"No, who?"

"I have a buddy in the Seventh Special Forces who knows who he was." Bishop replied as he scanned the rest of the ship

A man standing on the bridge of the Guevara was also holding a pair of binoculars and looking back at the Canadians. He looked nervous to the Corporal.

"Sir, drive on until you get to the stern of the next ship, then make an about face and head straight for the Guevara," Bishop ordered as he ducked below into the radio room. From there he could watch what the man did through a small widow in the tight cabin.

Scott was curious and the Corporal sounded adamant so he complied. When the Vergil was even with the next parked ship he had Mike bring the boat about and head for the loaded freighter.

As Bishop anticipated, the man disappeared into the ships wheelhouse and seconds later the gangway along the ship's side used to allow passengers to get on and off began to rise. The ploy had worked because Bishop had used it before. Make the enemy think you're not interested and then turn dead on like thunder. If they spook they're guilty of something.

In a few minutes the Vergil would be alongside and inspection of cargo for contraband would begin.

CHAPTER 20

"What Intel do we have on that Guevara ship Kirk?" Bishop asked.

Kirk who was manning the radios shifted some reports around and then pulled out a binder. Inside was a listing of all the ships supposed to be in the harbor, and those who were coming and going?

"Same ol' same ol'" Kirk said as he looked at the two page document.

The form was set up to tell of the ship's crew, captain, usual cargo, owners, and a list of ports it had been to in the last twelve months. It also included classification, what kind of cargoes it was allowed to carry, weights of the ship, and several incidental facts that together gave a clear picture, at least for the present of the ships makeup. Most of the information would change once the ship left port. Correspondingly, it listed times and dates of where the ship was while on its course from port to port.

"What's this?" Kirk said as he looked at a small entry at the bottom of the page. "See Probate."

"What's that?" Bishop asked.

"The ships been cited for something, I'll check it out but don't get too excited. They probably didn't flush the toilet the last time it was inspected," Kirk replied as he took out another binder, this one green in color, and thumbed through the pages until he found the ships name at the top.

Bishop glanced through the small window and could see they were getting closer to the Guevara.

"You want to check this one out Corporal," Scott called down through the open door.

"Yes sir, I got a feelin' about it."

"Right then," Scott replied and slowed the Vergil's speed.

"So what's it say?" Bishop asked now focused on Kirk.

"A couple of inspections ago they had painted over the inspection view windows into the holds."

"So?"

"The view ports are supposed to be clear so we can see what's in the hold."

"So they're hiding something?"

"It could be but usually it's because the cargo they carry has to be sanitized and there for the hold has to be clean. So they put a dozen coats of paint on the inside to keep the cargo from spoiling during transit. That's all it probably is."

"What's she carrying Kirk," Scott called down.

Kirk flipped back to the cargo manifest and called back, "Grains from BC sir."

"B.C.?" Bishop asked.

"British Columbia, they're bringing over aid for exchange. They'll probably take rice back."

"You two down there topside now!" Scott barked and the two came up to the bridge.

Once on deck Bishop could see they were only feet from the side of the freighter and about where the gangway would be if it was in its proper position.

Mike did an excellent job of keeping the Vergil in a hovering mode while Scott took up the bull horn and ordered the gangway down. Several tanned faces of Spanish descent appeared over the railings above them but it didn't look like the message was getting through. Scott made a second demand and this time a round whitish face appeared and waved down to them.

"Must be the bloody Captain, he's going to be trouble," Scott muttered.

A squeaking sound feel upon the small boat as the gangway was lowered. A lot of rust does that to delicate equipment not properly maintained.

"Kirk, get the small arms out, everyone gets a gun."

"Right sir," Kirk replied and dropped down into his little cabin and unlocked the arms cabinet, taking out four pistols he came back up and handed them out. Each man holstered his weapon and waited for the stairs up to reach its proper height above the water.

"You'll need this sir," Kirk said as he handed Scott the ships report, it was a duplicate.

"Right, now listen up. I'll deal with the master you two take a look inside and check out the holds for anything. Mike keep her close alongside."

The three men each hopped onto the metal stairs that ended at the main deck of the freighter. From there they would go their separate ways.

*   *   *

The Guevara was made up of three huge cargo bays covered with steel loading hatches at the main deck level. The only way in was through the hatch which had to be opened with the crane the ship already had on board. Between each cargo bay was a twelve foot wide space used to separate the cargos and keep them from being contaminated for whatever reason. This was also the inspection passage and to get into each compartment Bishop and Kirk had to climb down a ladder from the main deck to the bottom of the ship, about twenty five feet.

The bridge, where the ship's Captain made his domicile and office was two flights up from the main deck. To reach it Scott had to climb a couple of ladder ways to reach his intended target. Once on the bridge deck he entered the wheel house where he was met by the First Officer of Spanish origins and the round whitish face of the Soviet, non-English speaking master.

Kirk led the way because Bishop wasn't familiar with the layout of the ship. The deck hands; all three of them surrounded the two and followed along like geese chattering away in Spanish. They didn't look threatening and they were about eight inches shorter than the two Canadian's.

There was a small round hatch, just large enough to wiggle through on the main deck between the cargo bays, this lead to the passageway between the bays. Kirk turned the dog ears and opened the cover and looked down into the darkness. Reaching under the rim he felt around until he found the switch that turned on a couple of low watt light bulbs.

Like a belly dancer shaking her way out of her dress, Kirk performed the opposite gyration and lowered himself through the opening until his feet touched the first rung of the ladder. Carefully he slithered down and disappeared into the darkened passage. The Corporal followed performing the same maneuvers until the two were out of sight by the deckhands. When Bishop was a half dozen rungs down he looked up and spotted the faces of the three men staring down, but the difference between the daylight and the passage light made it impossible for them to see him.

At the bottom, Kirk was already trying to find the inspection window and when he did began to rub on the glass.

The window was wet from condensation buildup. The humidity inside the passage was extremely high because of the heat wheat will give off when piled into an enclosed space. The warmth was transferred through the bulkheads into the passageways and the cool of the deck above collected the moisture like rain. So much so the deck they were standing on had puddles on it.

"What do you think?" Bishop asked when he came up behind the Seaman.

"It's painted alright. Must have two or three coats on it."

"Okay, I guess that answers that." Bishop replied casually as if he had shrugged his shoulders.

"What's that?" the Corporal asked as he walked to his right toward the ship's hull.

"Inspection door into the compartment," Kirk replied as he followed closely behind.

Bishop looked over the doorway; he could see that it had been permanently sealed.

"Fucking things welded up tight."

"That's not unusual," Kirk replied.

"Aren't you supposed to get through?"

"Normally yes, but because this ship was built for hard cargo and is now carrying soft they need to keep the access doors dry. So they weld it shut."

"Why?"

"Well Corp," Kirk began like a teacher admonishing a student for not finishing his homework. "When you got say cars in here, if the ship flounder's the added water mixing with the cars doesn't add any weight. But if it's cement or flower, or in this case wheat, when water mixes with it, the cargo weighs ten times as much. Therefore the ship sinks like a stone with no time for the crew to get off."

"Okay Einstein, I got it," Bishop said as he turned and went back to the ladder.

Kirk followed and when the two were at the base, Kirk spotted a fire extinguisher in its cradle and couldn't resist checking the tag for the last inspection date. When he tugged on the tag the empty extinguisher fell on the deck and made a hell of a clanging noise. The container rolled across the deck and struck the cargo bulkhead making a second round or ringing.

Bishop, looking disgusted walked over and picked up the fire retarder and was about to hang it up in its carrier when he did the strangest thing. He let the extinguisher swing in his hand and hit the bulkhead again. The sound was the same, but it shouldn't have been.

"Huh," Bishop said softly.

Looking up the deckhands had disappeared knowing they weren't needed and probably took a smoke break at the railing.

"What's up Corp?"

This time Bishop held the extinguisher firmly and just tapped the side of the bulkhead a couple of times. The sound had a ring to it that seemed to echo on the opposite side.

"If that cargo bay is full of wheat, shouldn't that be a different sound?"

Kirk looked curiously at the wall and then replied, "I'd say so."

Bishop placed the device back in its holder and the two climbed up to the main deck.

*   *   *

Once out of the passageway, the two Canadians stood for a moment observing the ship.

The crew had left and for a moment the ship looked deserted. Glancing over the side Bishop could see Mike keeping the Vergil close to the gangway. He waved down and Mike responded accordingly.

"This doesn't look right Corp."

"You got that shit straight."

"Is there any way into that hold?"

"Not without taking the cover off and we need the boom for that," Kirk replied as he pointed to the winch and crane at the base of the mast. "What do you want to get in there for anyway?"

"I don't like the sound of hollow wheat." Bishop replied then added, "You see Scott anywhere?"

"Nope, but I'd suspect he's in the Captains Quarters, that's where they keep the log book and stuff." Kirk replied.

"I think we should pay him a visit."

Bishop pulled his pistol out of its holster and let it hang at his side. He turned the barrel into his bulky shorts so it couldn't be seen easily.

"Come on," Bishop said and the two walked slowly to the ladder way that took them up to the wheel house.

It was then they heard Scott's voice as he thanked the First Officer for complying with the inspection. The Russian Captain wasn't to be seen.

"You can breathe now," Bishop whispered as the two watched Scott descend to their position.

When Scott reached the main deck the three walked over to where the gangway was and paused to discuss the evidence. Scott had learned that the combined intellect of the group was much more useful than trying to make a single determination. It was painfully obvious he couldn't remember everything.

"What's the story from the bridge sir?" Kirk asked.

"The ships leased through a container company out of Hong Kong, probably a third party deal. It was originally owned by some company in Finland and then somebody in the Middle East had it, Egypt I think."

Kirk looked at the paint on the wheelhouse. It was badly faded green, the color used by companies shipping through the Suez Cannel. The green was a clear pass color indicating the company that owned it had been certified and registered through the International Oceanic Regulatory Service out of London England.

"That checks with the paint sir." Kirk said.

Scott glanced at the wheelhouse too and concluded the summation.

"There aren't any adverse entries. The dock to dock record is right, but there seems to be a problem in time between BC and here."

"What kind of problem?" Bishop interjected.

"She lost two days getting here."

"Yup, I'd say that's a problem but what's the tip off?"

"Well the log book is in order but I noticed that the arrival customs stamp was two days off when she arrived here."

"It's a rotary stamp sir, maybe customs didn't advance it or it was on a weekend," Kirk said.

The reference Kirk made was to the port of entry stamp. It had a series of numbers on a rubber band that rotated and any day, month, or year could be set and then stamped on the destination form.

"It was set for Wednesday, two days ago."

"Well that shoots that down the tubes," Kirk said, then thinking of something that could be used to cross check he asked, "How much fuel they got?"

"Just over four tons."

Kirk then leaned over the railing and called down to Mike. "Hey! What's the water mark read?"

Mike glanced at the column of numbers painted on the side of the hull indicating the ships draft. It told of how low in the water she was.

"Twenty six feet plus."

Kirk waved.

"Right, so she's carrying nineteen thousand tons, plus fuel and ship she should be riding around twenty two feet," Scott said as he ran the numbers through his head. There was a formula that had a few additions and subtractions to it, but it wasn't complicated. This made reference much faster even though the actual numbers may tell a slightly different tail, but only by a ton or two.

"Then she's over weight sir," Bishop pointed out.

"That's my guess too sir," Kirk added.

"It will take weeks to sort out the paperwork. What did you two come up with?" Scott asked.

"We might have something sir. The cargo bay is hollow down stairs," Bishop said boldly.

"Not down stairs Corporal, below."

"Sorry sir."

"We rapped on the bulkhead sir, there was an echo."

Scott paused and looked up at the wheel house. He spotted the First Officer watching them, but he didn't look threatening. There was no sign of the Captain.

"Did you check the cargo vents?"

Kirk snapped his fingers, "No sir, but that should do it."

The three walked over to the main cargo bay in the center of the ship. It was the bay they had recognized as being erroneous. Kirk found the snorkel like device that let air into the cargo bay so the contents wouldn't corrode. During bad weather the deckhands had to manually close the vents so sea water wouldn't leak in.

Rotating the cap, Kirk pulled it off and a slurry of wheat flowed out and made a cone on the deck. Kirk blew into the opening to see if the wheat would flow back away from the vent. But it didn't.

"It's right to the top sir." Kirk said with a grin.

"That means she was loaded not long ago."

"How can you tell?" Bishop asked.

"When the ship left BC she was loaded and during the crossing the ship sways side to side. That means the cargo settles and can drop as much as six feet from the top."

"I get it."

"Put the cap back on and let's get outa here," Scott ordered.

Kirk complied and the three quickly exited the ship.

As the Vergil made a turn back to base Scott surveyed the rest of the ship. It didn't look out of order, but that was the outside.

CHAPTER 21

I t wasn't that much, Major Tennyson thought after purchasing his ticket on the double decker bus. They even took Canadian money in Hong Kong, which for a foreign country says a lot about its confidence in western trade markets.

Taking a seat on the upper level he was able to see all of the action as the bus made its way down Liberty Avenue toward North Point Park, a destination every tourist insists is a must see. Because this was the older part of the city, the streets were very narrow and the four floor buildings created a canyon effect. This trapped noise, smells and lighting from signs within the confines and if it hadn't been for a stiff breeze off the ocean the place would have been unbearable.

What the transit director decided many years earlier was that the bus service was going to be allocated to tourist's only. Commuters weren't a consideration simply because most of them lived close enough to work to walk the short distance.

Subsequently, all the bus routes were of a circular design passing most of the points of interest within the British sector occupying the mainland part of the city.

Hong Kong was like Berlin before the Russians built the wall. The French, British, Chinese, and some Portuguese had taken over sections of the city with the onslaught of refugees from nearly everywhere in the South Pacific. When the Allies divided up Berlin they used streets to set the boundaries, but Hong Kong used rivers and so these small unofficial colonies began to thrive on each island.

Tennyson had called his pal at the British Foreign Trade Office and they decide to meet casually on the bus as tourists. The Major laughed at the pretense that Richard, his pal still played the spy role, even though Richard was nothing more than a salesman now dealing in the clothing markets to London.

For the rest of the off-the-record delegation from Hanoi, which included Roth the Assistant Embassy Director, Lock, Director of Foreign Agricultural Studies and a couple of clerks that needed a vacation, they had gone directly to their hotel, 'The Embassy', after arriving at the airport.

Roth's mission was described in a poorly written freehanded letter from Ottawa asking that he attend two functions on Agricultural machine sales worldwide being hosted by the Dutch contingent of the United Nations. Roth thought it ludicrous that such a small country with little to know use for heavy machines were the ones making the pitch, but then diplomacy was filled with strange bedfellows.

Mr. Lock on the other hand was glad to get out of Hanoi if only for a short breather. He and his functionaries were tied up with the North's persistent arguing about debt payments to Canada. He was told not to argue too much and just try to get some idea as to when Ottawa could expect the reimbursements. What was funny was just after he took over the posting he came across his predecessors notes and discovered this arbitrary merry-go-round had been playing out for more than four years.

When Tennyson made the statement he was going shopping alone, Roth nearly stepped out of his shoes. He never thought Tennyson was a man who liked to roam the streets at night looking for a gift for his wife back in Trenton. But after all, the Major was still a soldier.

It was near sunset and the buildings were bathed in a yellowish hue that made the colored lights used in advertising more than brilliant, but arousing. The people were dressed in evening wear that made the atmosphere more congenial. It had been stated that the British sector of the city was much more advanced because of the capitalism that was prominent everywhere. But some argued that the outside territories could make you blush as well.

From his seat Tennyson could smell the different odors that lunged toward the street from inside the various merchants shops. The smell of fried fish, rice, pork, silk, bread, coffee, and hundreds of other tantalizing aromas mingled with engine exhaust from motor cycles, taxis and mostly buses. To sum it up, it was a adenoidal feast for a schizophrenic indulger.

The bus turned a corner and came to a stop across the street from a branch of the London Exchange Office. It was obviously a scheduled stop and Tennyson paid little attention to it. The rows of empty seats gave him a clear view down the street and he could see the tree lined avenue that paralleled the Park. It was at least a mile on.

From the stairwell up popped a familiar figure, it was Richard dressed in a gray business suite with a red, white and blue stripped tie. He was in his forties but still carried himself like a professional still in service. Richard was carrying a travel map that had been folded a few times to make it look like it was being used.

"Long time no see old friend," Tennyson said as Richard slumped into the seat ahead of the Major.

The pal turned slightly as if he was going to engage in conversation and brought the map up as if he was going to point something out on it.

"Yes, it has been. About six years I should think."

"Right, I don't want to hold you up, but I've got a problem I need help with."

"You know I can't arrange things like before, I can only ask a few favors be drawn in."

"Yes I know," Tennyson said firmly. The Major had worked with the spy before and nearly got killed, but the lasting impression was like a free pass for him to engage Richard in anything speculative. "I've got these East Germans hanging around in Hanoi and asking questions. They even congratulated one of my officers for helping to bring in some big wig plant in the South."

"Interesting, any written notification?"

"No only verbal."

"Right then, it must be a small ops from God knows where, but it sounds like a side show."

"Well I thought so to. But they arranged to have an American newspaper print an article about this contact being captured in the South."

"Did they say anything about who did the capturing?"

"No but it's obvious the CIA's Phoenix program was involved somewhere."

"So how did they know it was your officer?"

"Well, he is a bit inexperienced and he's only been on the job for six months or so, but he got some letters from a Northern customs man and forwarded them down to Saigon via our diplomatic pouch."

"Good God, the man isn't inexperienced, he's an outright idiot." Richard proclaimed.

"We don't get the best out here like we used to."

Richard nodded and held the map up as if he were looking for something.

"As for these East German's; any clues why they're in Hanoi? I'm guessing it hasn't anything to do with the WARSAW PACT?"

"No, they're civilians as best I know."

"Well they could be in the trade industry, you know the North does a lot of business with Russia and that includes the Germans," Richard said shifting in his seat and adjusting the map. He then added casually, "What's your interest in this?"

"Well with the invasion going on we're handicapped as far as getting good intelligence and it would be helpful for us to do business with these Germans if we can trust them."

"You can't trust anyone old man, not even your mother."

"I know all that, but there's something to this. I get the strangest feeling they're on our side."

"Well we have one thing going for us, if they aren't on our side they would have turned your man in."

"Yes, that has occurred as well."

"Right then, when are you headed back?"

"Next Wednesday I've been told."

Richard began to rise out of his seat and then fell back into. "I just had a nasty thought."

Tennyson leaned forward; the noise from the traffic was beginning to intervene. "What?"

"These Germans may have already turned you in, and left your man out there to see what other bigger fish they could grab. Something like this could be big problems for Canada."

"I never thought of that."

"Why do you think I got out of the spy business, couldn't bloody tell who was on whose side anymore."

"Then you'll have to be discreet won't you old boy?" Tennyson said with a grin.

"Yes well, discreet is one thing being the bate is quite another," Richard remarked and climbed from his seat and walked toward the stairwell to descend to the main level.

Tennyson watched the man wobble away. Richard had to hold tight to the hand rails for balance as the bus rolled from side to side. The colored lights of the city surround the spy in a aura of red and blue. It made Tennyson think of better times.

CHAPTER 22

The bar of the Embassy Hotel was one of the most spectacular lounges in Hong Kong. It once hosted the Prince of Wales when he was on a worldwide tour. It was well known in the security circles as being one of the most difficult to protect because of the many ways in and out that couldn't be covered easily. Police stand out like sore thumbs in crowds and so do men dressed in tailored suits from London's High Street.

Roth decided, even after his ten PM night cap, that not knowing where Tennyson was made him nervous. He tended to be overly protective when on a jaunt and this made for a great deal of angst with the underlings as they too had to stay up. To ease the tension, he decided to do a walkthrough of the lounge which also gave him a chance to see all the pretty people as it were.

The interior of the elevator was walled in smoked glass and as he stood waiting for his floor he casually glanced into the darkened mirrors. Dressed like a hippy of sorts, flower shirt, tan slacks and hair in disarray, he briefly thought of his days as a college student at McMaster University.

Hamilton was a busy city and around the campus there was a neighborhood that blossomed by way of migrant artists. The college wasn't an art school but for some reason these degreed students felt they had found a home of some kind. Toronto wasn't more than fifteen minutes up 401 and it was a hard city to get used to. Besides that, it was too expensive for those with Art majors and no experience, even those who had taken graphic designed were by passed in the hiring circles.

But for Roth, he had acquired a taste for the arts, especially one artist in particular. She was a blonde from Manitoba, the big sky type, and having a business conversation with her was like pulling teeth. But she was one heck of a cook and that's what brought the two together. Unfortunately, business and art went its separate ways after graduation and new horizons, especially back in Manitoba, were too strong to ignore. Particularly when father wrote the checks.

The small conveyance bounced a bit when it reached the requested level and the doors slid open as if the jerking motioned unlocked the latch. Roth stepped out and into a wash of suite cases and a trolley loaded with trunks and travel bags. The thick piled carpeting gave him an added spring in his step as he walked toward the Mandarin Lounge.

As he remembered from the after dinner drink, the place was somewhat less engaged. The bar was lined with elbow benders all seeking a quickie before bed, and the overdressed ladies of action had begun turning down the allurement regulator.

There was no sign of Major Tennyson so Roth decided to head back to his room, but just as he turned to go he spotted Lock in a corner beside a large fern in an oversized terracotta pot. If he didn't know any better he would have thought Lock was hiding from someone.

"What's the matter can't sleep?" Roth said as he sat down across from Lock.

"No, I'm waiting for someone." Lock replied shyly.

"Who?"

"Her names Naomi, at least I think so."

"Oh come on now, you're not really going to buy a hooker are you?"

"She says she can give me a discount after midnight."

Roth leaned back in his set and was grinning from ear to ear. "You do know that if you catch something here they won't let you out of the country until you've been cleared by the consulate?"

"Well if that's what it takes to keep from going back to Hanoi I'll be here for the duration."

"Government employees don't make that much money."

"Says who? Besides, what else am I going to do with it?"

"You know this could go on your permanent record?"

"Doesn't matter, they tore down the high school years ago."

This entire conversation would have been very humorous if it wasn't for the fact Lock was serious. Roth hadn't had many dealings with the junior minister and didn't realize how much stress he was up against.

"We've got a breakfast meeting with the Dutch tomorrow. Don't stay out late," Roth said as he rose from his chair and went back to his room.

When Roth got on the elevator he turned in time to see a familiar face walking passed just as the doors were closing. He reached out to interrupt the sealing but was too late and had to ride the transfer to the top and back down.

When the return trip was completed Roth exited and headed for the lobby thinking the man was still in the area. When he didn't encounter the stranger he went back to his room. On the ride up he tried to remember where he had seen the man and that's when it occurred to him. It was one of the Germans who had been at the combine demonstration a few days before.

What the hell was he doing here, Roth asked himself and the answer was combines. For a moment he felt a bit more relaxed when he realized the situation would accept such a person and as Germany was very close to the Netherlands, why wouldn't he be here? Then Roth remembered that he was from the East German Agricultural Ministry and the problem was solved.

Feeling more assured, Roth went back to his room and called it a day.

CHAPTER 23

L ock had moved from his table to the bar, a lonely spot he picked out near the doors to the kitchen. The oriental foods being prepared seemed to hit his senses so often he was feeling full as if he had already eaten. As the hour neared mid night, and the lights in the room became dimmed to the point you couldn't see across the room, Lock decided to give Naomi one more chance to show up. Optimists engaged in the pursuit of pleaser are usually disappointed and he was no exception.

Lock was growing sleepy and blamed it on the inferior Scotch he had been drinking. He slumped in his chair, but he looked more distracted than he really was. It was then a man sat down beside him.

"And how are you doing mister Lock?" the man asked casually as if he had just met an old friend.

"I'm sorry sir, I don't know you," Lock replied in a somewhat sedated manner.

"Oh Ja you do. I was at the combine demonstration in Hanoi the other day. You remember I talked to you after the Americans shoot at us."

Lock began to squint at the man, there was something about him and the accent was a definite give away. "I think I remember now."

"Ja, you see you know me."

"You're with the German Agricultural something or other."

"Ja, that is right. I'm Werner Munnt," the man said as he held out his hand.

Lock reciprocated and the two seemed to slump together as if they were old drinking buddies.

When the bartender arrived Munnt ordered his Cognac and bitters. It wasn't an appealing recipe, but it didn't keep him awake at night.

"So you're here for the Dutch parade eh?"

"Dutch parade? Oh yes, I was sent here to just watch things you know."

"Got some damn breakfast I have to go to in the morning."

"There will be many there?"

"I guess the usual bunch of money hungry bankers. Everyone wants to get paid for something."

"You are not a banker," Werner said with surprise, he knew Lock from a file the CIA had on him.

"I know but Ottawa wants me to put the pressure on."

"For what?"

"The North is way behind in their payments and that's bad."

"But Canada is giving lots of aid to the North so I am told."

"Oh yea eh, they got some rubber stamp credit card with us, but how do we collect from someone who claims their broke."

"And are they?"

"Look buddy, the North has more money than you can shake a stick at. They just don't want to give it up I guess."

"There are other countries involved. The Chinese, the Russians, even us."

"Yea right, but that's all rice in the bag eh. Nearly every grain that gets sent out of the country the Chinese have dibs on it for the next twenty years. That's how they keep getting their missiles and stuff for the war."

Werner had learned loose lips sink ships and nothing could be closer to the truth in Locks case. So with the opportunity starring him in the face Werner proceeded to gather whatever he could.

"But rice isn't currency Ja?"

"Oh but Ja it is." Lock retorted with intent. "It's gold to the southern pacific nations."

Lock took another drink and glanced around the now empty bar room. It was late and he knew it.

"So the North converts rice to cash yes?"

"Not really, they get loans from other nations even us."

"How, they have to have collateral yes?"

"No they don't deal that way."

"Then how?"

"Sorry old chum, but I've about had it," Lock said as he rolled from his chair.

Werner sat upright as if he had just been insulted by a Dutchman. He pivoted in his chair to stay looking at Lock.

"We must talk again Ja."

"Right, maybe I'll see you at breakfast eh."

"No, I'm not invited, but maybe lunch yes?"

"Right on, see you then," Lock said holding his fist up in a symbol of white power.

Werner watched the Canadian stagger away, but by the time Lock reached the end of the bar he had found his feet and was walking like someone who really needed a lot of sleep.

The East German began to wonder if he had found a contact of influence.

CHAPTER 24

He had left the damn garage door open again, Captain La Rouch said when he looked out the window of the chateau and seen the black Lada was gone along with the Groups only NCO. Even on Saturday's it was imperative that company procedures be followed, but Sergeant Wilkins was a man the Captain gave leeway too. It was mostly because of his rank and position in the Group.

"Has anyone seen Wilkins this morning?" La Rouch asked the three man group around the dining table.

The Captain had entered the mess during the men's breakfast hour and took his place at the head of the table. He reached for the plate of scramble eggs and began to deposit his portion when Ed spoke up.

"Yes sir, I saw him leaving about zero seven hundred. He didn't say where he was going but I figured you must know about eh."

"I suppose he's off doing embassy detail again," John, the cook added.

"The old Sergeant still gets around. He was with the Major the other day." Bill added with a wink just as La Rouch looked at him.

"You're not supposed to know this but the Major has put him in for his crown," La Rouch muttered as he began to eat.

"Wow, promotions in this outfit. I never," Bill said with a grin.

"Yes," La Rouch said. "It's pretty rare when you're off the reservation. But I suppose the Major knows what he's doing."

"Under regs' sir, the Major is authorized to have a Master Sergeant for an aid." Ed added authoritatively.

"I guess," the Captain replied.

"Well that means we're going to need a senior NCO now that Bishop ain't here anymore," Bill said.

"So why don't they bring Chief Warrant Harper up from Group 2 to hold the Majors hand," John asked to anyone who would answer.

La Rouch was crunching down on a piece of toast, so Bill answered instead. "It's because all the Groups need an officer in charge and Harper is as close as you can get in a pinch eh."

"Besides, I would guess that Group 2 is getting plenty to do down there."

"I heard on CBC yesterday that the Americans are fighting back and the North has stalled out eh."

"Yea, it's going to be butt kick time before long," John said.

"Hey sir," Ed asked. "Have you heard anything about what the guys down in the South are up to?"

"There was something about a bunch coming up as far as Da Nang, but nobody coming here to Hanoi."

"Probably the North won't stamp their pass ports eh," John added with a laugh. It got the group chuckling for a few moments. The laughter was a good release.

La Rouch had forgotten about Wilkins for the moment. The dialog around the table brought out too many topics of concern. Although most of the infractions to the Cease Fire Agreement were being committed way down south and with the trailing off of bombing raids by the Americans, life around town was coming back to normal. But there were plenty of opportunities for things to go wrong without prying into old wounds.

*　　*　　*

By the time breakfast was over at the Group, Wilkins had driven out to Mai's house, picked her up and were well on the way to the Village of Tri Ping. Once passed Vinh Gai Bridge that had been closed due to bombing, the five mile detour took them close to another small village Mai had visited as a child. She knew of a place to stop and get something to eat and drink, and Wilkins, who was always ready to take nourishment, was easily persuaded to comply with her wishes.

It wasn't a regular restaurant of any description, only a small house with two rooms and a large canopy over the back patio. The small tables were arranged so there was a view of the rice paddies in any direction, but the mountain backdrop was an added touch of grace.

With the car parked on the side of the building somewhat out of sight from passing police, the two made their way inside and took up residence at one of the empty tables. The sun came out and the warmth was as much appreciated as the food that followed.

"This is going to add time to our trip," Wilkins said as he took a sip of tea.

"Not much, the decoy bridge is just a mile or so on," Mai said.

"You know about this area eh."

"Oh yes, I lived with an uncle just down the road from here. The house is gone but you can still see where it was."

"What happed to your uncle?"

"He was killed fighting with the Viet Cong a few years ago."

"I see; did they bring his body back?"

"No, but there is a marker at the church where we can burn incense to him." She said sadly.

It had become a tradition by the North's government to allow the catholic population to maintain some churches for just this reason. The Buddhist had also dedicated rooms for the small empty urn representing the remains and to be held on a small shelf for respectful visits.

The food arrived and they began to nibble away at the fruit and tea. A small cake of bread had been provided but there was no meat. For the price, it was a hardy meal.

"How are things at the hospital; are they getting any easier?" Wilkins asked to break the quiet.

"We are seeing a lot of soldiers now. Only the worse cases. It's hard you know, I see the families crying in the halls and it's difficult to not be . . ." Mia's voice started to crack and he could see the stress levels starting to climb.

Wilkins finished the sentence, "Moved."

"Yes," Mai said as he looked down at her bowl. She didn't want the man to see her emotions welling up.

Wilkins rose and went around to her, he reached down and pulled her to her feet and held her.

He couldn't relate to what she was feeling, as a soldier who had lost buddies before he learned to never get close to anyone for just this reason. As a result he was a lot like Bishop who also practiced restraint of emotions. He could feel himself tighten up inside. It begins in the gut and goes to the chest. It becomes hard to breathe because you think you're having a heart attack so you simply try to relax. You try to hold the building pressure inside and if you're lucky you won't cry.

She clung to the tall Canadian like a drowning man holding onto the only flotation device left. Wilkins could feel the heat from her body as it worked to hold back the tears, but like a dam that can't hold back the flood; she broke down and started crying uncontrollably.

Slowly he moved her back down into her chair. He reached over and grabbed the back and swung his chair around beside hers. He sat and held her even tighter because he was now losing it himself. The two were in a seated embrace.

They were locked together in emotional bounds that surpassed any other kind of feeling. In most relationships gestures are motivated by a need, but when someone is caught up in the misery of life, gestures are meaningless. Instead, a true connection to those experiencing grief is brought about by the sincerity of touch.

For a moment they became one and the pain was shared. This is what some mistakenly take for advantage, and as a result only make things worse. But Wilkins wasn't that type. He genuinely felt her pain and he too was being brought in.

He reached down and drew his beret out of his belt and wiped his face, it was the only hanky he had. He then moved her away slightly and tried to dab the tears from her cheeks.

Mai pulled a cloth from under her uniform jacket and blew her nose, ever so lightly. It was as if a gentle wind had brushed away the due.

"You okay now?" he asked. He held her close but left enough room for her to move about. She seemed small like a child to him, and it was a new feeling.

Mai nodded and whipped her nose, and then moved out of his embrace. She straightened herself as if her commanding officer had just entered the place.

Wilkins got up and moved his chair back to where it was and resumed his meal.

For a moment he felt lost. He had just been a part of an experience that only two people could feel and yet it was like it never happened. He coughed to clear his throat and he began to feel much more at ease, yet she seemed to become more reserved. He thought about her internal fortitude and how strong it must be to react from one extreme to another without a sense of transition.

It was then he looked up and saw her smiling at him. Her face was still reddish and her eyes were glistening from the tears not yet recovered. And again she seemed to be smaller, like a child who had just cut her knee and been given a sucker as a reward for not crying. In his mind he flashed back to many scenes he had observed of children, after being hurt are suddenly excused from the horror to the sublime of rescue.

Mai took a sip of tea and said, "We should go, long way yet."

Wilkins smiled his reply and stood up. He seemed to tower over her, but he didn't mind.

She led the way out as if they were merely friends chatting at whatever life had given them recently.

Once in the car, Wilkins pulled out onto the road and drove toward the decoy bridge. She leaned closer to him and he wanted to put his arm around her, but the situation wouldn't allow it. How would it look to a guard if a Polish Sergeant who only spoke English was hugging a Northern soldier?

CHAPTER 25

Wilkins thought how uncanny it was for Bishop to intuitively know the roads to the village as well as Mai who had to give him directions. There were parts of the road he recalled and some of the villages they drove through had some essence of recollection, but if he had to do it himself he knew he would have ended up in China.

The Lada was hard on gas and so Wilkins was directed to some farms along the way that gave them enough gas to make it to the next refueling point. The reason they stayed off the main road was to be as clandestine as possible. Wilkins dressed like a Polish paratrooper and Mai like a nurse in the North's Army wasn't that unusual, but any chance of questions being asked was avoided at all costs. At the same time, each refueling place asked no questions because of the authority they looked like they possessed.

They were about twenty miles from Tri Ping, after just crossing Route 6 and picking up a secondary road when the gas gage read empty again. Wilkins knew he had at least enough gas to make the village but Mai wasn't sure there would be any fuel to be had because of the restricted supplies caused by the invasion. That was why they went to farms because Mai knew all the farmers kept some extra gas around.

They decide to take a chance and get back on Route 6 now that they were in Dien Bien Phu district and make for a large village. Wilkins was nervous but Mai kept talking about some of the places she had played in and was pointing out various houses where her old friends lived. In some ways it brought back memories of his youth and the cities and towns he had lived while growing up. A completely different landscape, but the principle of the memory was predominant.

Mai had managed to direct him to a small road that came up just inside the town limits and the main road was just ahead.

"Which way do I turn?" he asked curiously.

"To left, only a couple houses down."

Wilkins made the turn without stopping, there wasn't any traffic so the maneuver was executed smartly. When he straightened out he spotted a Shell gas sign and pulled in.

"You pump, I pay," Mai said as she exited the car and walked toward the small building that looked derelict for the last century or so.

Wilkins climbed out and began cranking the hand pump which brought the gasoline up from a large in ground storage tank. Electricity had yet to make it to ALL the villages and towns even in 1972. Although the communist party had made several speeches on the subject, the required response was the paperwork hadn't gone through yet.

Mai came out of the shop folding some change and slid it into her back pocket. She walked proudly and came around to stand beside Wilkins, both stood watching the slowly dropping bubble in the clear tube signifying how much gas they were getting.

It was then that some middle aged man came across the street carrying a Polaroid One Step camera. He walked straight up to the couple and held up the camera, the grin on his face was his welcome card.

Mai waved a finger at him as if to warn him off, but Wilkins, for some strange reason reached over and grabbed Mai around the waist pulling her to him. He smiled at the man and nodded. Mai, who was startled at first began to conform to the frolicking and settled into him like an old friendly chair.

She smiled and the picture was complete. The man snapped the shutter and the whirring sound deposited the print. He tore it off the end of the camera and blew on it helping the negative to dry into a full color photo.

"There," Wilkins said. "We have a souvenir."

Mai reached out and gave the man some money and then drew the picture close to her as if she was cherishing it. She was smiling when Wilkins looked into her eyes, and he wanted to kiss her, but she pulled away, like a kid on the school grounds.

"Here, you take, you keep," she said jokingly.

The man turned and went back the way he came. Wilkins replaced the hose from the pump and then took the picture. He smiled and slowly tucked it into his shirt pocket.

As they drove from the gas station Wilkins glanced at the shop the man had come from and noticed he had hundreds of pictures posted on the walls outside the building. A large metal roof covered the area so the pictures wouldn't get wet.

"That's weird," he said.

"What is weird?" she asked.

"That man has bunches of pictures on his walls."

"Not weird, he keeping record of who live here and come through town. That way if someone go missing they have picture to start hunt with."

Wilkins smiled and drove on, picking up speed as they left the last house in town in the rear view mirror. He wondered if it was going to be necessary for anyone to have a picture of them to start the search for.

CHAPTER 26

He would miss lunch but that couldn't be helped. Captain La Rouch was anxious about something and he didn't know what. Since he awoke that morning something was gnawing at him. While sitting on the side of his bed he tried to segregate good from bad thoughts thinking it would help for him to put his finger on the problem, but nothing seemed worthy of investigation. He had taken the blue pickup and decided to take a drive around the city with no particular destination planned. La Rouch determined that a ride through familiar territory would heighten his awareness to the stomach pain and there by zero in on what may be wrong.

His first turn brought him out on the river road just down from Chong Dung Bridge that was the only vehicular bridge that crossed the Red River in Hanoi. The railroad bridge a half mile up had been converted to auto traffic and in one direction. It was only used after the American's had bombed the highway bridge.

The Chong Dong had been on the target list for US bombers for years and there was a standing order, that if any American was to go 'downtown' he'd better be sure he dropped at least one bomb on that bridge or he would never fly again.

With this in mind the North's engineers decide to build the bridge in segments. That way if one or two segments had been destroyed they could easily drag out new segments and replace the damaged ones.

In fact, unknown to the US the North had built a warehouse a half block up river from the bridge where they stored the segments on pontoons. The outside of the warehouse had been painted to look like a large cluster of shanties and a market complete with people standing around. A pilot traveling at high speed would only see a blur but his mind would fill in the blanks and he would assume it was a regular part of town.

When the attack was over the segments would be rolled out into the river and floated down to the bridge where they were installed. In most cases the bridge was only out of service for three hours.

La Rouch was about to pull out into the flotilla of motorcycles and trams when a black Chaika drove passed accompanied by a couple police jeeps. They went screaming past so quickly the Captain barely had time to react and get stopped. He watched the short convoy disappear into the collection of small vehicles and noticed the brake lights never came on.

When the way was clear he proceeded out and drove toward the citadel, headquarters for the North's military. He didn't know why he just followed a hunch. Perhaps it was because of Wilkins and Bishop helping with the disposal of the bomb that landed there earlier in the month, or just curiosity.

He had to stop for cross traffic entering the bridge and as he pulled up short he spotted the turn off that went toward the East Gate, where he met Horst and he was congratulated for his sending Ho Buc's letters to his wife. He drove passed the turn and kept going.

La Rouch scanned the railroad bridge as he went by and kept following the crowd that started thinning out. Before he knew it he was on a large highway with the river on one side and a large lake on the other. He became aware of the area in his mind as he realized he was close to Major Tennyson's quarters. He recalled the sailing club with only a half dozen boats for rent and a pagoda on a small island in the lake that looked to be more in distress than the victims it was supposed to save.

For a moment La Rouch started feeling strange. It was as if he were in some kind of travel brochure and expecting to see a fast food restaurant or Texaco gas station at any second. There was a sense of euphoria beginning to build within him. The war was an afterthought that had faded into the past and he was now on an outing he usually enjoyed back home in Vancouver. Glancing into his rear view mirror he could see the dark mountains west of Hanoi and he put in his mind that they were the Rockies, only smaller.

The Captain began to think of his family, his young brother who had just graduated high school and was contemplating military life. He thought of how neat it would be if both served in the same unit, only in a more peaceful place like Gibraltar.

The road became clear of traffic as he left the city behind. The usual Saturday market goers were already in town and that meant the countryside was wide open.

He crested a small hill and as he began to come down the back side he slowly pressed down harder on the gas pedal. The speed steadily increased. The speedometer read forty five, then fifty, then sixty, but the Captain had not bothered to concern himself with the device.

In his mind he was slipping into a motion causing trance. He could see the road was open and he began to feel relaxed. It was like looking into a telescope and only seeing dark shapes way off in the distance. The shapes had no discernible connection with each other and yet the mind was busy trying to organize them into something distinguishable.

It was about this time that he started seeing flashes far ahead. It wasn't gun fire or headlights but something bright like sun bouncing off glass. It wasn't steady either, it came and went but with no synchronization. The countryside flew passed but he had no feeling of it, and his body began to feel warm, something he hadn't experienced since monsoon started.

What caused him to break through these strange feelings was he began to wonder about what was really happening. The cognizant side of his mind was slowly over taking the false reality he had conjured up. Then the road began to widen and his vision began to expand to include the upcoming disaster.

There was a muffled bang in the rear of the truck and the steering wheel began to shutter like it was about to come off in his hands. His mind flashed into the present and he suddenly realized he had a high speed flat tire, but he wasn't losing control of the truck. He then spotted the parked bus filled with peasants that blocked his way and he swerved to miss the loaded vehicle.

The truck dashed into the shallow ditch beside the road, then flung itself out and went end over end through a farmer's front yard coming to a smoking lump of metal just yards from the buss.

There was a moment of silence as those looking on who had witnessed the one vehicle accident came out of their trances and began to cluster around the wrecked truck. The blue paint and UN painted on the door did little to expedite rescue of the driver.

It was then a small fire began near the engine compartment. The flames grew rapidly, and those stout hearted men ran forward to see where the occupant was. But before they were even close enough to look inside, the truck exploded and landed another twenty feet away from the bus.

CHAPTER 27

For a former Stasi agent, Ellermann was as sophisticated as a dead horse when it came to observation or the shadowing of foreign dignitaries. At least the ones he knew about which included commissar Schenko.

When Ellermann was a Major in the East German State Security Directorate, his job was to track down and bring to trial dissidents that were pro American or British. He was also Jewish which made him work harder to prove he was completely committed to the East German State and the Communist Party in particular.

As he rose through the ranks on the merit of his ambitions in arrests, he also made several enemies. He also made a friend, a General Stiger who wasn't Jewish, but had some sympathies in their direction.

What Stiger saw in Ellermann was a man who was very much like a young college student that had been killed by the KGB when Russia put down the Hungarian Revolution in 1956. That man's name was Ekman and he was not pro-Western, but in fact he was pro-Russian. He just happened to be home when the MVD, the Soviet Armies Intelligence and forerunner to the KGB, broke into his house and arrested his father. Ekman tried to resist along with his father and both were shot trying to escape.

At the time Stiger was a young Lieutenant in a special pre-invasion force that went before the regular troops to get information on possible resistance fighters that would be a problem. The fighters were determined by those who were avoiding possible arrest themselves and offered information, however false, that would put them in a better light with their new Soviet masters. Stiger, who learned later that Ekman wasn't a dissident, nor his father, made a personal obligation to try to right a wrong by helping out those who carried Ellermann's cross.

But there was one inconsequential case that put Ellermann's carrier in jeopardy and at the time Stiger was also brought under the microscope. This somewhat exacerbated betrayal of intelligence lead to nothing, but someone had to take the hit and Ellermann was to be the obvious choice. Stiger intervened and if he hadn't Ellermann would be serving time in a gulag somewhere.

So it was decided that Ellermann be banished to North Vietnam as a transitional observer. This meant even a janitor could order him around. Stiger, on the other hand was promoted.

It was just before lunch when Ellermann was called to Dmitri's office for an update of his snooping missions. It was a reluctant Dmitri that led the meeting but it was a required regulation by the Politburo so he complied as he should. Being a temporary Soviet representative, he couldn't get out of it.

The two chairs by the widow was the site of the exchange and for a brief moment sun light blasted the area, causing Dmitri to place a hand over his eyes to see the former Stasi agent, and it appeared as though Dmitri was permanently saluting the East German.

"And what was this about Commissar Schenko at the airport all about?" Dmitri asked in an uninterested manor.

"Sir, he was trying to by a date with one of the stewardesses from Lao Air."

"Was she good looking?"

"Ahhh a bit heavier than most."

"Good legs then?"

"Like a fisherman's wife sir."

"What I don't understand was how he planned to get this Laotian woman back to Moscow without his wife knowing about it."

"I believe he was going to employ Diplomatic Privilege sir."

"So how did it end?"

"She had to go back to Lao's sir. Her husband the pilot insisted."

"I don't suppose he could have got her on a later flight?"

"No sir, you know how clickish these Orientals are."

"Da, that's why I never married,"

"Is there anything else for me sir?"

"Just one thing, I have been informed by Moscow that some kid of accident has taken place up by the northern border with China. Two men died in a mud slide and apparently some Soviet equipment has to be replaced. A water pump or something. Moscow just want's an idea of what needs to be sent to them."

"But isn't that an internal matter sir. I'm not with Agriculture."

"I know that, but I'm not sending what few people I have to some God forsaken river gorge for probably nothing. That's why your here anyway, isn't it?"

Ellermann paused; he knew he had no recourse but to follow orders. It was only a few years off, but retirement was going to be a blessing after all this.

CHAPTER 28

They were about a block away from the building that had the dud bomb in the front yard, a picket fence surrounded the site. Pogo grinned as he watched two civilians tip toeing away from the area. He thought about how ridiculous it was. At this point a tank couldn't set the thing off.

"Rope is secured comrade sergeant," Private Conneski said as he dropped the line.

The Polish EOD unit had managed to find some of the North's craziest soldiers to work with them. Pogo had decided to use them as a reserve force, doing the grunt work as it were, while he and his men did the disarming of the dub bombs.

The Pol's had gathered a substantial amount of expertise in the process of removing the American's accidents. The US embassy had designated the term 'accident' to any munitions that failed to explode. Obviously, they claimed, it was an accident because it failed to do its job.

The scene was one of typical despair, a narrow avenue surrounded by several buildings of varying heights most over three stories. The local was across the river from downtown in the Binh An District, once marsh lands filled in and then buildings were constructed. It was after the French left so most of the structures were of the late 1950's and early 60's design. It was somewhat modern; but still looked old from the debris of bomb fragments that feel on it.

The street was vacant except for the red EOD truck and a new Soviet UAZ jeep. That was the vehicle the North's men used. What was nice about it, it had an enormous amount of pulling power and could yank any thousand pounder out of the ground in one pull. The rope, Conneski had dropped was connected to the jeeps hitch at one end and the tail fins of the bomb at the other. This was the usual setup once the bomb had been defused. But this was one of the newest bombs in the Americans arsenal and the Pol's hadn't deactivated it yet.

"It hasn't got the removable card like the others, "Pogo said to Urlink, his Czechoslovakian tech man.

The two men had become very close because Urlink was smarter than most lumpers, and he had given advice in the past which had saved lives. This made Pogo a hero to some, and Urlink was rewarded by Pogo keeping him off any special duties the KGB had thrown at them on occasion.

"Could the access door be at the back with the fuse?" Urlink asked.

The two men were standing at the rear of their red truck and a shelf had been built to use as a work bench. On it was a fuse from another bomb that Pogo kept looking at to see if he had missed something.

"Nie, there was nothing there, only yellow paint on the fins and fuse ring."

"May be they knew it was a dud when they dropped it. Like yesterday in the market."

"That was different. The Americans have a nasty sense of humor, but the one's that work on this shit don't kid around like that."

"What are we going to do?"

"I wish the Captain was here, he would know."

"The comrade Captain was sent home last week. Moscow will send someone else out."

"Tak and we will have to train him as well."

"Sergeant," Urlink said firmly as if he knew everything. "The KGB has evidence of Captain Zimbowski sending counterfeit money home to his wife. He had thousands of Rubles in his office."

"KGB make that up, they want Zimbowski out; he make them look like idiots," Pogo argued as he tossed a wrench into the tool box that had been sitting unused. "You remember when we do paint on American bomber? They make Zimbowski stay back so they can watch him. He didn't do anything. Besides, how would Captain be tied to counterfeit money? That was KGB making stuff at North's base up river."

"Who didn't do anything comrade sergeant?" A voice came from behind them.

Pogo and Urlink turned to see a Colonel in the KGB standing just a few feet away. The man was dressed in a black leather waist coat and black fedora, a relic of the old days, but to the Colonel it was a keep sake from his wife back in Moscow.

Pogo instantly recognized the officer from the fake air base they had built with the B-52 and MIG positioned together. It was the propaganda ministries best mockup of a captured bomber.

"Sir!" Pogo said and snapped to attention. Urlink did the same while the North's men just sat in the jeep and watched with grinning faces.

"What is taking so long with this bomb Sergeant?"

"I was about to get back to work on it sir."

"Nie," Urlink added. "We just making sure it is safe to move."

"And is it?"

"Not yet sir. It's a new type we haven't seen before," Pogo said as he tossed the fuse back into the cargo box of the truck.

Instantly the fuse made a hissing sound like air escaping from a balloon. A small cloud of vapor rose up and quickly dissipated.

Pogo looked at the Colonel who was expressing a substantial amount of fear.

"Don't worry sir," Pogo said jokingly. "That is only gas that makes bomb explode, but it has to be under pressure for it to work."

The Colonel straightened himself and looked down the street. He could see where the rope went across the fence and then disappear. The hole that the bomb was in was made wider as the EOD men shoveled out the mud to make room to work.

"What does it look like, this new type bomb?" The Colonel asked; his voice started to shake a bit, as if his mind was on something else.

"Like all the rest comrade Colonel. But it hasn't the extra defusing part. Or at least we can't find it," Urlink responded.

Pogo looked at the Colonel for a moment and tried to remember where he had seen him before. Yes he was at the fake bomber site and yes he had been around their base and Zimbowski's office. Pogo then recalled that when the Captain was sent home it was rumored that the Colonel was going back to Moscow to appear at the phony trial the Captain would have just before they sent him to prison.

"And the rope?"

"We were going to pull out bomb to see what was underneath. If it goes off we won't know what caused it."

"I think I would like to see this bomb before you do that," the Colonel's voice was becoming more distraught. The color seemed to flow out of his face. "I was an EOD man during Korean War. I might teach you a new trick."

Pogo looked at Urlink and the two were secretly saying the same things to each other without sound. The Colonel was playing at something, but what?

It was going to be risky, but Pogo had to do something. Zimbowski was a friend and they had served together for many years off and on. But most importantly, the Captain was Polish.

"Comrade Sergeant," Urlink said as he tried to double guess the NCO's motives.

Pogo stepped forward and stood beside the Colonel. The Pol had a trusting expression on his face.

"Your Captain would want me to see it Sergeant," the Colonel said.

There was a silent transference going on between the two men. It was unspoken because of obvious reasons, yet each new there might only be one result.

The Colonel walked over to a tool box and took out a short shaft sledge hammer. The two NCO's could hear it scrape across the metal lid.

"We go yes?" the Colonel said with his hand extended in an invitation.

Pogo stepped up beside the officer and the two walked slowly down the street keeping the rope between them. It started to rain slightly. The drops made a snapping sound on the Colonel's leather jacket.

CHAPTER 29

"**D**id you know your Captain was making counterfeit money and sending it home Sergeant," The Colonel asked as they strolled toward the front yard of the house.

They walked slowly, each step paced exactly matched to the other man's gate.

"No comrade Colonel. How would I know of such business?" Pogo replied softly. He was growing impatient.

"It was mentioned that you and the Captain were very close and the office thought you might know something. Anything that might help the Captain's case yes."

"The Captain is a fine officer sir. I'm proud to have been a member of his parachute regiment."

"Yes, yes, we have heard all that before and I congratulate you on your loyalties, but they may be misplaced in this case."

"Sir, I don't have anything to add to my opinion of the Captain.

They took a couple more steps and the Colonel glanced over at Pogo in a condescending way.

"We know some things about you too comrade sergeant."

"I wouldn't be surprised sir. The KGB has always been overly efficient organization." Pogo was starting to see the plan. The Colonel wanted him to confess to as much dirt as could be gathered and then the Sergeant was to commit an honorable suicide by striking the bomb with the sledge hammer. This was always the way the KGB got rid of problems. As for the Captain he would be sent to Siberia no matter which way it went.

"As a matter of fact Sergeant we know that you have been stealing our uniforms and selling them to the Canadians."

"They are not your uniforms sir they are Polish uniforms. I know this is true but it is a Polish problem and nothing to do with Moscow."

"Yes you are right, but the Lada you gave to them. You know where that car is right now?"

"What Lada sir, we had one that was destroyed and we sent the parts back to Cracow."

"Come, come, sergeant, the car is being driven by your friend in the Canadian Army and we last saw it going out of town this morning." The Colonel said and then paused in the middle of their walk. The street was still very empty and only the sound of the city hum could be heard in the wind. The rain had held off, at least for the moment. "Doing business with the enemy is a capital offense, and that puts Moscow in the picture. The other stuff, uniforms, all that is nothing."

"I have not done business with the enemy comrade Colonel and I won't admit to it ever."

They started to walk slowly on and were about half way to the yard. The very end of the bombs guidance fins could be seen over the top of the fence.

"You were present at the freight station the day the printing press arrived here in Hanoi, weren't you?"

"Yes sir, you were there also and you know my men and I helped with the moving of the machine and its cargo."

"And you know the Captain was in charge of security for the equipment yes?"

"I wasn't aware of such orders sir. And Captain Zimbowski never told me of this."

"But you knew he would be involved somewhere yes?"

"It was my understanding sir that you were in charge of the shipment. And it was you who gave us our instructions sir." Pogo was growing nervous, but he had learned to keep it under control.

"Do you know what was made with that printing press Sergeant?"

"How would I know that sir? The last time I saw it; it was in the basement of a bombed out freight station."

"Your Captain made money with that press Sergeant. Lots of Rubles and other currencies."

Pogo paused; they were within fifty feet of the yard now and more of the bomb could be viewed, somewhat nervously. This information, if it was accurate would condemn the Captain in any court, no matter how bent it was.

"I never saw the Captain do this work sir."

"Oh course you didn't, he was doing it behind everyone's back, including yours."

"So if you have the evidence, what do you need me for?"

"You are a good friend of the Captains and you Pol's stick together. I understand this yes, but you know an officer is more important than an NCO. It is quite possible that your Captain could be reeducated in the proper political ways and serve out his time with distinction."

Pogo turned to face the officer. The colonel hefted the hammer up onto his shoulder as if he was about to go off to work with it. Pogo starred into the man's lifeless eyes, they were gray and watery. A true mark of a coward that gets things done without untidy ends.

"And so I'm to do what sir?"

The officer reached inside his jacket and pulled out a single page of white paper. It was folded in two and was printed on one side.

"I'm to go to Moscow next week and report at your Captain's hearing. I think if you were to sign a statement that says you're involved and the Captain was merely duped by you into holding onto the money we found in his office, that the court would be more lenient."

Pogo reached out and took the paper, opening it he saw that it was written in Russian and he couldn't read it. The only thing he read that was understandable was his name at the bottom of the page and a line under it.

Pogo's heart nearly stopped. His chest muscles had contracted and it felt like a heart attack, if that was what it was supposed to be.

He couldn't believe it was to end this way. He had performed his duties and even went beyond the normal channels, but it was harmless. And what of his family in Canada, would they be left alone. He didn't dare ask for clemency for them, even though they had migrated many years earlier and legally. The KGB didn't confine itself to legalities.

The Colonel could see he had the upper hand, and the Sergeant, being a good soldier would follow orders, even if they were implied. He reached into his coat pocket and pulled out a pen, clicking the end to expose the ball point. It was an American pen, the kind that had two different colors to the barrel.

Pogo took the writing device, and then paused as if something had struck him the wrong way.

"Sir, can I ask you where you got this pen?"

"What difference does it make?"

"None of course, except that how would you have an American pen?"

"It's not an American pen!" the Colonel argued.

"But it says PARKER on the side."

"Sign the paper Sergeant."

It was then that a car came rushing down the empty street right passed the red EOD truck. A black Soviet made Chaika followed by two military police jeeps loaded with the North's finest.

The car screeched to a halt as the Colonel let the hammer drop off his shoulder and land with a thud at his feet. He turned to face the dozen men in black suites and leather jackets rushing toward him.

But before they got close the Colonel whirled around and got behind Pogo and yanked Pogo's right arm behind his back. He drew out a pistol and shoved it into Pogo's neck on the left side.

The men stopped and drew out their weapons pointing them straight at the two.

A solitary man that looked all to proficient in that sort of thing stepped forward with his hands in his pockets of the long coat he was wearing.

"Comrade Colonel," the man said with determination. "You know why we are here."

"This man is an enemy of the state; he must be arrested at once. I have his confession."

Pogo, who was still holding onto the paper dropped his hand and shoved it into his pocket. The pen fell to the street.

"Colonel, you are under arrest."

"For what, I haven't done anything wrong."

"That is for others to decide, now come along peacefully."

There was a moment of silence between the parties, and it was interrupted when Urlink and the others came running up but stopped about thirty feet away.

The Colonel began to panic and he was shifting Pogo's body from one side to the other. But the Sergeant was feeling the weakness of the Colonel and took advantage. He shifted his hips to one side and shot his fist into the Colonels groin. With his left hand he knocked the gun from his neck and broke free.

The Colonel was bent over and landed on his knees in the street. He was in pain and Pogo was about to kick him in the face when the man yelled halt.

Pogo stood over the Colonel and looked so angry he could spit.

"That is no way to treat an officer of the KGB Sergeant," the man said as he stepped up and was looking down on the man in pain.

Pogo leaped back when the shot was fired and went through the back of the Colonel's head. A whiff of smoke leaked out the hole in the man's coat pocket.

"No way at all for a Colonel to act," the man said and turned and went back to the car. The other agents that had come lurched forward; took up the lifeless body of the Colonel and stuffed it into the trunk of the Chaika.

The North's finest merely sat and watched the entire show without flinching.

Pogo wet over to the car and looked through the spotted glass window. "Sir, what about Captain Zimbowski?"

"You will see him again I think," the man said without any hesitation. Then added, "Get rid of that paper in your pocket."

"Yes sir," Pogo replied as he stepped back and watched the parade of vehicles leave.

"You know they will send out another one don't you?" Urlink said with contempt.

Pogo glanced at his assistant and replied, "Then the Americans should start dropping bigger bombs."

BOOK FIVE

BISHOP'S CANIVERS

COMING IN SPRING OF 2013